Joseph Le Brandt

My Lady Darrell

Joseph Le Brandt

My Lady Darrell

ISBN/EAN: 9783337118969

Printed in Europe, USA, Canada, Australia, Japan

Cover: Foto ©Raphael Reischuk / pixelio.de

More available books at **www.hansebooks.com**

My Lady Darrell

OR

A STRANGE MARRIAGE

A Drama in Four Acts

BY

JOSEPH LeBRANDT

NEW YORK
HAROLD ROORBACH, PUBLISHER
132 NASSAU STREET

MY LADY DARRELL.

CAST OF CHARACTERS.

ALICE, *afterwards Countess of Darrell* . . . . LEAD.
VIOLA VAUGHN . . . . GENTEEL HEAVY.
LADY DARRELL, *Roy's mother* . . . . . . STRAIGHT OLD WOMAN.
MARTHA PAISEY . . . . CHARACTER OLD WOMAN.
KATE CRIPPS . . . . EMOTIONAL HEAVY.
MOTHER CRIPPS . . . . CHARACTER OLD WOMAN.
LORD ROY DARRELL . . . . JUVENILE LEAD.
GEORGE VAUGHN, *alias Count Jura* . . . . . GENTEEL HEAVY.
ARMSTRONG DALE . . . . LIGHT COMEDY.
SIR GEOFFREY RAWDON . . . . STRAIGHT OLD MAN.
CAPTAIN LIONEL WYNDHAM . . . . JUVENILE MAN.
JOSEPH PAISEY . . . . CHARACTER COMEDY.
JOB TROTTERS . . . . CHARACTER COMEDY.
TOBY BRUCE . . . . CHARACTER HEAVY.
DALTON, *Sergeant of Police* . . . . UTILITY.

TIME. — The Present. PLACE. — England.

TIME OF REPRESENTATION. — TWO HOURS AND A HALF.

NOTE. — This play can be produced by ten persons (six men and four ladies) by making the following particularly easy doubles.

{ LADY DARRELL.
{ MOTHER CRIPPS.
{ CAPT. WYNDHAM.
{ JOB TROTTERS.
{ TOBY BRUCE.

{ MARTHA PAISEY.
{ KATE CRIPPS.
{ JOSEPH PAISEY.
{ DALTON.

or { ARMSTRONG DALE.
{ JOB TROTTERS.

2

SYNOPSIS.

ACT I. — *Scene* 1. The Paisey Farm. "Now, strike if you dare!" *Scene* 2. Lord Darrell's Estate. A Strange Marriage.

ACT II. — A lapse of four months. The Plot. The Insult. The Blow.

ACT III. — The Abduction. The Recognition. "You are the murderer of Capt. Wyndham!"

ACT IV. — In London. "I'll rescue her, if it takes the last drop of blood in my veins!" The Beggars' Paradise. Finale.

COSTUMES.

ALICE. Act I. — Common gingham gown, with sunbonnet. Act II. — Handsome house-dress. Act III. — A handsome silk wrapper; slippers. Act IV. — Very ragged dress. In make-up and choice of colors, she should contrast sharply with VIOLA.

VIOLA. Act II. — Handsome house-dress. Act III. — A tightly fitting morning-gown. Act IV. — Dark street dress, hat, and heavy veil. She contrasts in coloring and make-up with ALICE, — one blonde, the other brunette.

LADY DARRELL. Act II. — Handsome house-dress. Act III. — A pretty wrapper. Iron-gray hair.

MARTHA PAISEY. Act I. — A common calico dress; handkerchief about neck; sleeves rolled up. Act IV. — A common dress of cheap goods; bonnet and shawl.

KATE CRIPPS. Act III. — A dark red dress, with fancy kerchief about neck; bright red kerchief tied around head; large earrings — a very gipsy-like appearance. Hat and jacket. Act IV. — Same as before, except that she wears a bandage on her head instead of the kerchief.

MOTHER CRIPPS. A dark woollen dress, very old and faded; small shoulder shawl; hood. She has straggling gray hair, with pale make-up. Looks like a witch.

ROY DARRELL. Act I. — Shooting costume; fore-and-aft cap; boots. Act II. — Evening dress. Act III. — Black cutaway coat and vest; light trousers. Act IV. *Scene* 1. — Same as in third act. *Scene* 2. — Beggar's disguise; viz., ragged coat, trousers, flannel shirt, and slouch hat; false full beard (on wire).

GEORGE VAUGHN. Acts I., III., and IV. — Dark, shabby suit; slouch hat. Act II. — Evening dress.

ARMSTRONG DALE. Act I. — Shooting costume similar to DARRELL'S. Act II. — Evening dress. Acts III. and IV. — Black cutaway coat; white vest; light trousers.

SIR GEOFFREY. Act I. — Shooting costume similar to DARRELL'S. Act II. — Evening dress. Acts III. and IV. — Black Prince Albert coat and vest; dark trousers.

CAPT. WYNDHAM. Shooting costume similar to DARRELL'S. Or he may wear the undress uniform of a British officer.

JOSEPH PAISEY. Act I. — Rough gingham shirt; straw hat; rough trousers stuffed into boots. Act IV. — A cheap suit, rather loose and ill fitting; paper collar on gingham shirt; soft hat — he should look like a farmer in his best suit, which has had considerable wear.

3

JOB TROTTERS. A cheap suit much too small for him ; " high water " trousers ; very small derby hat with a very narrow brim ; paper collar; very gay necktie.

TOBY BRUCE. Rough coat and trousers — velveteen, if possible ; coarse shirt ; red kerchief about neck; cap. He has about a week's growth of beard.

DALTON. Regulation " Bobby " uniform

PROPERTIES.

ACT I. *Scene* 1. — Tablecloth and black snake whip for MRS. PAISEY. Novel for ALICE. Wheelbarrow, pitchfork, paper and pencil, for PAISEY. Bouquet and long paper (poetry) for JOB. *Scene* 2. — Shot-guns for ROY, DALE, WYNDHAM, and SIR GEOFFREY. ROY'S gun has a loop of wire attached to the trigger, for JURA to catch hold of. ROY'S gun should be cocked before he enters ; great care, therefore, should be exerted to prevent a premature discharge and possible accident. Small basket, covered with white cloth, for ALICE. Watch and pocket-flask for DALE.

ACT II. Furniture as per scene-plot. Pictures, bric-à-brac, etc., to dress the stage. Small bell off R. 3 E., to strike the hour. Cases of jewels and bouquet for ROY. Card and pencil for JURA.

ACT III. — Bag containing silverware and cases of jewels for TOBY. Fire-wood for MOTHER CRIPPS. Loaded revolver for JURA. Candle in tin candlestick, lighted, on table L. C. Key for JURA. Diamond ring to give MOTHER CRIPPS.

ACT IV. *Scene* 1. — Locket and carpet-bag for PAISEY. Valise for MRS. PAISEY. *Scene* 2. — Dish-pan, containing potatoes and potato-knife, for MOTHER CRIPPS. Placard " Help the Blind," shade for eyes, wooden leg, crutches and coins, for BEGGARS. Whiskey bottle for MOTHER CRIPPS. Coins for ROY. Diamonds in cases and loaded pistol for JURA. Some old quilts and rugs up stage. Candle in candlestick. Furniture as per scene-plot. Dagger for MOTHER CRIPPS. Red fire off R. 3 E.

SCENE PLOT.

ACT I. *Scene* 1. — Landscape drop in 4 G. Wood wings. Set house, with practicable door and steps, R. 2 E. Water-trough (half of a large barrel), 1. C. Pitchfork stands against house, above steps.

Scene 2. — Woodland, with wood drop in 4 G., and wood wings. Clear stage.

ACT II. — Fancy interior boxed in 3 G., backed with a garden or landscape drop in 4 G. Double door or arch C. in flat. Balustrade behind this opening, to represent a balcony. Doors R. 3 E. and L. 3 E., backed with interior backings. Door L. 1 E., leading to conservatory. Plants in pots near this door. Have heavy curtains or hangings at all doors. Sofa in centre of stage. Fancy table L. C. with small chairs R. and L. of it. Piano at L. 2 E. At R. 2 E. a small desk with chair in front of it. Just L. of these stands a screen behind which ALICE retires so that she is concealed from the C. of stage while remaining in full view of the audience. A mirror hangs against L. wall, or stands on piano. Small stands for

4

statuary or flowers, up R. C. and L. C. against the flat. Pictures, bric-à-brac, etc., *ad lib.*, to dress the stage. This set should be as handsome and tasteful as possible.

ACT III. *Scene* 1. — A plain chamber in 1 G. Doors R. C. and L. C. in flat.

Scene 2. — Gothic chamber in 3 G. Doors C. in flat, R. 3 E. and L. 3 E. Tack old red curtains over all the doors, and back each door with a dark (stone) backing. At R. 2 E. an old chair without a back. At L. C. an old table with a rickety stool R. of it. Three or four old wooden boxes up L. C., near the flat. Lights half down until climax ; then flash. Use candle during this scene.

ACT IV. *Scene* 1. — Street in 1 G.

Scene 2. — Den boxed in, 3 G. A rough kitchen will do, as the scene represents a thieves' den. If possible, raise the drop about four feet above the stage, letting the bottom rest on a bridge or platform. Door C. in the drop, with dark backing, practical steps leading down from this C. door. These steps should be firm, and have posts on each side, to which are attached hand-rails running up to each side of the door. Doors R. 3 E. and L. 3 E. with interior backings. Doors L. 3 E. and C. have practicable bolts. Boxes, barrels, rubbish, etc., about stage. Some old quilts and rugs on floor of stage, on each side of the steps. Old chair, stove, etc. Rough table, with stool L. of it, L. at about 2 E. Candle, burning in candlestick, on table. Lights half down.

ABBREVIATIONS.

In observing, the player is supposed to face the audience. C. means centre; R. right; L. left; R. C., right of centre; L. C., left of centre; C. D., centre door; R. D., right door; L. D., left door; D. R. C., door right of centre; D. L. C., door left of centre; D. F., door in the flat; C. D. F., centre door in the flat; R. D. F., right door in the flat; L. D. F., left door in the flat; 1 G., 2 G., 3 G., etc., first, second, or third grooves, etc.; 1 E., 2 E., 3 E., etc., first, second, or third entrances, etc.; R. U. E., right upper entrance; L. U. E., left upper entrance ; UP, up stage or toward the rear; DOWN, down stage or toward the audience; X., means to cross the stage; X. R., cross toward the right; X. L., cross towards the left.

R.   R. C.   C.   `   L. C.   L.

5

MY LADY DARRELL;

OR,

A STRANGE MARRIAGE.

ACT I.

SCENE.—The Paisey farm. For description of setting, see scene-plot. MRS. PAISEY *is DISCOVERED at door of house. READY* PAISEY, *with wheelbarrow, to enter* L. 3 E.

MRS. PAISEY (*appears at door, shakes table-cloth, and calls*). Alice! Alice! Drat the girl, where can she be? Alice, I say! (*EXIT, into house.*)   [PAISEY *is heard whistling, off* L.

ENTER PAISEY, L. U. E., *pushing wheelbarrow; he wheels it to* C. *of stage and sits in it, facing the audience; takes paper and pencil from his pocket, and begins to figure. He is very slow of speech and action, and drawls habitually.*

PAISEY. Six times nine — let me see, how much is that? (*Calculates on fingers.*) Fifty-four. (*Makes figures on paper.*) Now, four's a four. Six and five's (*figures on fingers*) eleven — one to carry — one and one is two. It's just as I said — there's no money in raising ducks; they eat more than what they bring, to say nothing of all the trouble of looking after 'em. (*Puts paper and pencil into pocket.*)

MRS. P. (*calls, inside house*). Alice! Alice! Oh, wait till I get her — I'll break every bone in her lazy body!

PAISEY (*looks slowly toward house*). That's my wife. Guess I'd better be moving afore she starts in on me. (*About to rise when* MRS. PAISEY *appears at the door; he sits again.*)

MRS. P. Oh, you're back at last, eh?

PAISEY (*meekly*). Yes, mother.

MRS. P. (*mocking him*). "Yes, mother." Where have ye been fer the last three hours? (*Comes down steps to* R. *of* PAISEY.)

PAISEY. Feeding the ducks, mother.

7

MRS. P. Feeding the ducks! Does it take three hours to feed seven ducks?

PAISEY. Well, mother, some of the ducks had wandered 'way off down in the meadow, and I had to drive 'em back.

MRS. P. Did it take three hours to walk down to the meadow and back?

PAISEY. Well, mother, you see the ducks was in the pond, and I had to wait until they come out on the bank. (*He has one foot crossed over the other, and is swinging it.*)

MRS. P. Oh, you lazy-bones, you'll make me lose my temper.

PAISEY (*aside*). I wish she would lose it, and find another.

MRS. P. Have you seen Alice?

PAISEY (*slowly*). No.

MRS. P. Do you know where she is?

PAISEY. No.

MRS. P. Oh, I'm all out of patience!

PAISEY (*aside*). She always is.

MRS. P. What are ye waggin' yer foot fer?

              [PAISEY *scratches his head.*

Now he's scratchin' his head. Don't scratch yer head.

              [PAISEY *starts to get up.*

Now he's gettin' up.

         [PAISEY *sits down. READY* JOB, *to enter* R. U. E.

Now he's sittin' down ag'in — he does it on purpose to aggravate me. (*Goes up stage and calls off* R. U. E.) Job! Job!

PAISEY. That's right; call Job. He's got lots of patience.

MRS. P. Job! Job, I say!

JOB (*off* R. U. E.). Yes, Mrs. Paisey, I'm comin'.

MRS. P. Yes, you're comin', and so is the judgment day. (*Comes down* R. *of* PAISEY.)

ENTER JOB, R. U. E.

JOB. Did ye call, Mrs. Paisey? (*Comes down* L. *of* PAISEY.)

MRS. PAISEY, R.   PAISEY, *in wheelbarrow*, C.   JOB, L.

MRS. P. I've been screeching this half hour. Did I call! Where is Alice?

JOB. I dunno.

MRS. P. Here's another bright one. Well, go find her, and tell her to be here in less than a minute, if she knows what's good for her. (*EXIT into house.*)

JOB (*looks after* MRS. PAISEY, *then at* PAISEY; *to* PAISEY). Your good wife seems in bad humor.

PAISEY. Good wife! I'd like to know what's good about her; and as for the bad humor, did ye ever see her in any other kind?

JOB. Well, she do make you stand around.

PAISEY. That she do; but she ain't to be compared with my first wife.

JOB (*surprised*). Why, be ye married afore?

PAISEY. Oh, yes; she was a tartar. (*Sighs.*) When she died, that ought to have been a lesson to me; but no, I must take another dose of the same medicine

JOB. What did she die from?

PAISEY. Eh?

JOB. What did she die from?

PAISEY. She died from home.

JOB. No, no; what was the complaint?

PAISEY. Oh, no complaint — everybody was satisfied.

JOB. What was the disease.

PAISEY. Oh, the disease? Well, I can't say exactly. Nothing serious.

JOB. Nothing serious — and she died of it?

PAISEY. Well, I tell ye; the doctors just couldn't seem to agree what ailed her, but 'tween you and me, she was a powerful talker — she took the lockjaw, and when she found she couldn't talk, it struck in and killed her.

JOB. Don't ye think your good woman is a little hard on Alice?

PAISEY. 'Tween you and me, I do; but where's the help for it?

JOB (*looks cautiously at house; then confidentially to* PAISEY). Well, Mr. Paisey, I've thought of a way — now if ye'll help me.

PAISEY. 'Course I'll help ye (*suddenly thinks, hesitates*), that is, if mother don't object.

JOB. We won't let your good woman know nothin' about it.

PAISEY (*astonished*). What! Keep it from mother, with her eyes and ears. (*Shakes his head.*) Ye don't know her.

JOB. Well, I don't think your good woman —

PAISEY (*interrupting quickly*). Now, Job, just oblige me by not callin' her my *good* woman.

JOB (*grins*). Jest as ye say. Well, she won't object after it's all over.

PAISEY (*puzzled*). After what's all over?

JOB. The marriage.

PAISEY (*still puzzled*). What marriage?

JOB. Why, mine and Alice's.

PAISEY (*laughs heartily*). Shô'! man? She won't marry ye.

JOB (*annoyed*). Well, I dunno why. I'm not so bad looking. (*Draws himself up.*)

PAISEY (*looking at him critically*). No; but ye'd never take a prize at a beauty show.

JOB (*as if arguing*). I'm a good dancer.

PAISEY. Ye look it. I'll be bound ye can raise the dust with them boots. (*Laughs.*)

JOB. Besides, I'll tell ye a secret. (*Confidentially.*) I've been a-buying her books to read.

PAISEY. What, them yaller back novels?

JOB (*proudly*). Yes; did ye see them?

PAISEY. Mother saw 'em; she built fires with the " Beautiful Wretch "; she made porous plasters out of " Dead Men's Shoes"; and she stuffed a hole in the attic window with " Three Sewing Girls."

JOB (*almost crying*). What! I always gets one new one fer every two I take back.

PAISEY. Well, ye won't take 'em back.

JOB. I'll give her a piece of my mind. (*Turns toward house, as if about to enter it.*)

PAISEY. I'd advise you not to; she said if she found out who brought them books here, she'd scald him.

JOB (*stops, hesitates, and looks at house*). Guess I'll let it go. (*Deprecatingly.*) I don't like to have words with a woman —'tain't good taste.

PAISEY (*in a decided tone*). No, not with *mother*. Well, Job, if ye can get Alice to say yes, I'll help ye.

JOB (*eagerly*). Ye will? Say, Mr. Paisey, it would take me an hour to thank you.

MRS. PAISEY (*appears at door*). Hain't ye gone yet, Job Trotters?

JOB (*quickly to* PAISEY). I'll just thank ye another time. (*EXIT quickly*, L. U. E. *READY to re-enter.*)

MRS. P. (*comes down steps to* R. *of* PAISEY). And as for you, get up and do something; get in the wood — it will soon be growing dark.

PAISEY (*with dignity*). Now, mother, I just want ye to understand that I'll move when I get ready.

MRS. P. What's that? (*Starts at* PAISEY; *he jumps up, and takes handle of wheelbarrow.*) I thought ye said ye wouldn't move till ye got ready?

PAISEY. Well, I got ready.

MRS. P. (*shaking her finger at him*). Now look ye, Joseph Paisey; lately ye seem inclined to put on airs and talk back. I'll gin ye to understand, once for all, what I say is law in this house, and I'll take no impudence from you. Job gins me none, Alice gins me none, and ye sha'n't gin me none.

> [*During this speech she has been trying to get at* PAISEY; *he has handles of wheelbarrow, and circles around stage, keeping barrow between himself and* MRS. PAISEY.

PAISEY (L.). Ye can talk, mother, but ye can't reach me.

MRS. P. (R.). Can't I? Just wait till I get that horsewhip — see if I can't reach ye.

> [*She makes a break for the house, and EXIT in door.* PAISEY *makes a break for* R. U. E., *with barrow. Just as he disappears behind the house, she comes out and makes a crack at him with whip.* PAISEY *bellows as if hit.*

(*Laughs exultantly.*) Caught him! (*Throws whip down near*

steps.) I'll show him who rules this house. (*EXIT into house, head held high*.)

PAISEY (*sneaks from behind house; shakes his fist at door*). Just wait. One of these days I'll get my temper up, and then — (*he is C. of stage*).

JOB (*running on*, L. U. E.). She's comin', she's comin'!

[*READY* ALICE, *to enter*, L. U. E.

PAISEY. O Lord! where? (*Starts to go*, R.; JOB *catches him*.)

JOB. There. (*Points*, L. U. E.)

PAISEY. Who do ye mean?

JOB. Why, Alice.

PAISEY (*sighs with relief*). I thought ye meant mother.

JOB. Now, you go keep your good woman away while I talk to her.

PAISEY (*almost screams*). What, go in the house with mother? (*Decidedly*.) No, sir; not for a fortin.

JOB (*imploringly*). Ye promised to help me.

PAISEY (*points to* R. U. E.). I'll just go around behind and peep through the windy. If she starts to come out, I'll holler.

JOB (*looking* L.; *lost in admiration*). My, ain't she an angel!

PAISEY (*looking at house*). Who, mother?

JOB (*disgusted*). No, Alice. Here she comes. (*Pushing* PAISEY, R.) Go, quick; I feel my legs giving away.

PAISEY. What, for fear of meetin' Alice? You ought to have mother to deal with. (*Slaps* JOB *on the back*.) Brace up, be a man; I'll holler. (*EXIT behind house*.)

JOB (*shaking as if he had the ague*). O Lord! She's here. It don't look as if she belonged on this earth — she just looks like one of them pictures of angels. I'm all of a tremble, as if I had the ague. (*Stands up stage a little* R. *of* C.)

ENTER ALICE, L. R. E., *reading novel; she does not notice* JOB, *but goes down* L. *and sits on watering-trough; reads a moment, and lets book fall in lap; sighs.*

ALICE. What a beautiful story! It seems as if, in a dream, I can see a beautiful house — a kind, loving face bending over me. I can almost feel a loving mother's kiss pressed to my lips, and hear a tender voice whisper sweet words in my ear. It is but a dream, but, oh, such a dream! I wish I could shut out the reality, and live on and never wake. (*Sighs; looks abstractedly at book in lap*.)

JOB (R., *has been trying to attract* ALICE'S *attention; comes awkwardly down* C.). Hem! Miss Alice.

ALICE (*looks at* JOB). Oh, is it you, Job? (*Smiles a welcome*.) I thought you had gone.

JOB (*laughs awkwardly*). No — I'm here. (*Hat in hand; offers flowers*.) I brought you a little bouquet. (*Pronounces it bucket*.)

ALICE. For me? (*Takes flowers.*) It is very kind of you to think of me. (*Still sitting on trough.*)

JOB (*bursts out*). Think of ye? Why, I'm always thinkin' of ye; I can't do anything else. (*Spouts.*) The rose is red, the violet's blue, them flowers is sweet, but not as sweet as you.

ALICE (*laughs*). Why, I declare, you are quite a poet.

JOB (*deprecatingly*). Oh, I writ that in a minute. I've got a longer one — nineteen verses — that's better; I'll read it to ye. (*Takes long paper out of pocket.*)

ALICE (*in alarm*). Not now, Job, some other time.

JOB (*puts paper in pocket*). Jest as ye say, Miss Alice; but it's awful purty — all full of darts and bleeding hearts. (*Fidgeting.*) Say, Miss Alice (ALICE *looks at him*), will you go to the Wilkins's party? I'm going to ask Mrs. Paisey if I can't take ye.

> [*When* ALICE *is not looking at him he braces up as if on the point of popping the question; when she looks at him his courage oozes, and he wilts.*

ALICE. I am ever so thankful to you, Job, but I think I would rather not go.

JOB (*disappointed*). Not go? Why, there'll be lots of fun — the whole neighborhood will be going.

ALICE (*hesitating*). Yes, I dare say it will be nice; but they drink, and are so coarse. They always make fun of my white face, as they call it. (*Appealingly.*) It isn't my fault, is it, Job, that I am not big and strong like the rest of the girls hereabouts?

JOB (*indignant; blurts out*). Your fault? White face? Why, you're a lady, and they — well, they ain't. They're jealous — it's sour grapes, that's what it is. You're right, they are rough. Why them Wilkinses girls, when they gets some beer aboard, ain't got as much sense as blind mules. (*Blusters.*) I'd just like to hear any one of them making fun of ye, it wouldn't be good for 'em. (*Doubles up fist threateningly, trying to be sentimental.*) O Miss Alice, if ye'd jest give me the right to purtect ye, I'd lay some on 'em out. [ALICE *looks at him; he wilts.*

ALICE (*quickly*). Oh, no, Job; I wouldn't like to see any of them hurt. (*Rises.*)

JOB (*admiringly*). Now, that's jest like you, Miss Alice. Do ye know, everybody loves ye?

ALICE (*laughs*). That's a rather broad assertion. Whom do you mean by everybody?

JOB (*starts bravely*). Well, your Uncle Joe and (*hesitates, then blurts out*) — and me.

ALICE (*surprised*). You, Job?

JOB. Yes; I wanted to tell ye ever so long, but I couldn't get up the spunk. (*Quickly.*) I love ye, Miss Alice, and if ye'll only say yes, I'll have the banns called next Sunday. (*With a deep sigh, turning partly away from* ALICE.) There, it's out at last.

ALICE (*comes a step or two toward* JOB). I am very sorry you have said this. (*Slowly.*) I can't marry you, Job.

JOB (*turns to her, entreatingly*). Don't say that, Miss Alice.

ALICE. I am sorry to hurt your feelings, Job, indeed I am ; you have been very kind to me,— one of my few friends,— and now I shall lose your friendship. (*Almost crying.*)

JOB (*blusters*). No, ye won't ; jest because ye won't marry me, do ye think I'm goin' to get mad and turn my back on ye? No sir-ee. I've been your friend, and always will be, an' if I kin ever do anything to prove it, ye just call on Job Trotters.

[ALICE, *almost crying, has been abstractedly pulling the flowers to pieces.*

Don't pull them flowers to pieces, Miss Alice.

[*READY* MRS. PAISEY, *to enter from house.*

ALICE (*realizes what she has been doing*). Forgive me, Job. I didn't know what I was doing. You will forgive me? (*Lays hand on his arm.*)

JOB (C.). 'Course I will, when ye ask me in that purty way. Why, I'll bring ye a bucket every day, jest to see ye pull them to pieces, and have ye ask me to forgive ye.

ALICE (L. C., *smiles*). Thank you, Job. I must go in, now. I am ever so much obliged for the flowers. (*Crosses toward house.*)

JOB (L.). Oh, don't mention it. They didn't cost me nothin'. (*Hat in hand ; laughs awkwardly.*)

ENTER MRS. PAISEY, *from house.*

MRS. PAISEY (*speaks from steps*). So, there you are at last (*Comes down* R. *of* ALICE.) Where have you been gaddin'?

ALICE (C., *meekly*). I have been in the grove, reading.

MRS. P. Reading ! And leaving me to do all the work (*snatches book from* ALICE'S *hand, and shakes it in her face*), filling yer head with this trash, dreaming yer a lady when yer an idle good-fer-nothing minx that eats us out of house and home ! If I find out who gives ye these books (*throws book off* R. 1 E.), I'll make it warm for 'em.

[*READY* PAISEY, *to enter* R. U. E. JOB, *who has been working himself up during* MRS. PAISEY'S *speech, and looks as if he were going to interfere, suddenly stops and goes* L., *when* MRS. PAISEY *threatens to make it warm.*

(*Exasperated, to* ALICE.) Why don't ye speak?

ALICE (*quietly*). I have nothing to say.

MRS. P. (*working herself into a rage*). Nothin' to say ! Yer fast enough with yer tongue when I find any fault with yer uncle — as if ye had any right to interfere between man and wife.

[PAISEY *has* ENTERED *during this speech ; he stands up stage, listening.*

I want ye to go on an errand to the castle.

ALICE (*quickly*).   To the castle?   O Aunt Martha, I am afraid; it will soon be dark.

MRS. P.   Afraid!   Afraid of what?   Honest people have nothing to fear.

PAISEY (*coming down* R. *of* MRS. PAISEY).   There, mother, let the errand go till morning.

PAISEY, R.   MRS. PAISEY, R. C.   ALICE, C.   JOB, L.

MRS. P.   You, Joe Paisey, shut up.   Who's attendin' to this, you or me?

PAISEY (*meekly*).   You, mother.

MRS. P. (*to* ALICE).   I say, to the castle you go, and to-night.

JOB.   Let me do the errand, Mrs. Paisey.

MRS. P.   Hoity, toity, so you want to interfere!   Job Trotters, attend to your own business; I'll 'tend to her.

JOB (*can control himself no longer ; blurts out*).   Yes, yer always 'tending to her, beating and abusin' her, and she a-takin' it like an angel, never sayin' a word.   You're an old — cat-a-ma-ran !

MRS. P. (*speechless*).   Why, you big, lazy lout, you're sacked from this farm.   You can't work for me from this night.

JOB (*working himself up*).   I'm glad to leave yer old farm.   Ye ain't satisfied to abuse her and yer husband, who dassen't say his soul's his own; but because ye can't do the same to me, ye starve me.   I ain't had a good meal since I've been here. (*Comes toward* C., *close to* ALICE.)

ALICE.   Hush, Job, you will only make matters worse.

JOB (*desperately*).   I won't hush.   I've had this in for a long time, and if I don't let it go now, I'll bust.

MRS. P. (*turns to* PAISEY, *who is laughing slyly at* JOB).   Joe Paisey, are yer going to stand there and see yer wife abused? Thrash that man.

PAISEY (*almost paralyzed with astonishment*).   Eh?

MRS. P.   You thrash him, or I'll thrash you.

PAISEY (*braces up and blusters*).   Look ye, Job Trotters, I'm not going to allow ye to talk to my wife like that.   Get off this farm. (*Looks at* JOB *threateningly*.)

JOB (*stands his ground*).   I'll go when I get good and ready.

[PAISEY *hesitates, and looks at* MRS. PAISEY.

MRS. P. (R. C., *threateningly to* PAISEY).   Remember what I said.

PAISEY (R., *threateningly to* JOB).   Get off the farm.

ALICE (C., *in alarm, to* PAISEY).   O uncle !

ALICE, *up* C.

MRS. PAISEY, R. C.   JOB, L. C.

PAISEY, *down* R.

MRS. P. (*to* ALICE).   You mind yer business. (*Urging* PAISEY *on*.)   Go for him, Joe.

JOB (*spits on his hands*). Yes, you jest go fer me. I can't thrash yer wife, but I can take it out of your old hide. (*Starts at* PAISEY, *who retreats toward house.*)

PAISEY, *near house.* JOB, R. C. MRS. PAISEY, C. ALICE, L. C.

PAISEY (*seizes pitchfork, standing against wing; to* JOB). Now, you git. (*Starts for* JOB; *he retreats*, L., *crossing in front of* MRS. PAISEY *and* ALICE. PAISEY *follows him up with pitchfork.*)

JOB (L.). Lay down yer weepon; lay down yer weepon!

MRS. P. (*coming down, behind* PAISEY, *to* R. C.). Go fer him, Joe. [ALICE *stands in alarm*, C.

PAISEY. I'll do it. (*To* JOB.) Ye git. (*Chases* JOB, *ad lib.*, *around stage, and follows him off* L. U. E.)

MRS. P. (*to* ALICE). Now, see what ye have done,— drove away a good farm-hand just when we need him most.

ALICE (*quietly*, C.). It was your temper that drove him away.

MRS. P. (R. C.). Don't answer back. What do I keep ye fer? Yer'e no good about the place.

ALICE. I suppose you keep me for my dear mother's sake, your sister.

MRS. P. (*who is almost beside herself with rage*). My sister! She was no sister of mine. Yer'e no kith or kin to me — you're a waif — a stray that we took in for charity.

ALICE (*shows some spirit*). My coming was the means of your getting this farm.

MRS. P. It's a lie! Who told ye that? (*Looks at her keenly.*)

ALICE. I heard Uncle Joe say so when you quarrelled with him yesterday. He said the money I brought with me gave him his start in life. My mother helped you, and the least you could do in return, would be to treat her daughter kindly.

MRS. P. (*in a rage*). Yer mother! It was my hard work that got this farm. No thanks to anybody. Yer mother, indeed! A good-for-nothing —

ALICE (*breaks in upon* MRS. PAISEY). Stop! You can abuse me,— you can beat, or even kill me,— but (*bravely*) I will not allow you to speak ill of my mother.

MRS. P. (*almost speechless*). You won't allow! Well, it's the truth — yer mother was like you, stuck up, nobody was good enough for her. She had to marry a gentleman, so she run away with one, a nobleman! (*Sneeringly.*) Nobleman, indeed! (*Almost hisses.*) When she crept back here to die, she had a child, but she had no husband — no father for you.

ALICE (*angrily*). It is false. Your husband has told me many times that my mother was a good woman. I believe him; my heart tells me that he spoke the truth. When you say such things, when you cast a blot upon her memory, it is cowardly. She is dead and cannot defend her good name; but I am her child, and I say it is a lie.

MRS. P. You hussy! to defy me to my face! I'll show you! (*Gets whip where she threw it on steps; about to strike.*)

ALICE (*quietly, but firmly*). If you strike me with that whip, I will go to the castle and appeal to Lord Darrell. I will repeat what you have said, that I am the daughter of a nobleman — probably one of his friends. He will not refuse to aid me. Now, then, strike me if you dare.

[*Picture: A dark change. Or drop the curtain long enough to clear the set house, watering-trough, etc., and change landscape to a wood in 4 G., with wood wings. Clear stage.*

ENTER SIR GEOFFREY RAWDON, R. 2 E., *laughing, followed by* ARMSTRONG DALE.

SIR GEOFFREY. Dale, you are positively the worst shot I ever saw. I verily believe you couldn't hit the proverbial barn door. (*Laughs heartily.*)

DALE (L.). Laugh on, laugh on; you may get into trouble some day. I may be engaged as the other fellow's counsel, and you will find that I won't miss when I fire an avalanche of invectives at your head.

SIR G. (R., *banteringly*). If you don't make a better lawyer than you do a hunter, I'm sorry for your clients. (*Suddenly thinks.*) By the way, how have you been progressing during my absence? Have you any hope of a brief in the near future?

DALE (*pompously*). Oh, bless you, I have tried my first case!

SIR G. (*with interest*). Indeed! What kind of case?

DALE (*off hand*). Murder; I appeared for the accused.

SIR G. Well, I suppose you cleared him?

DALE (*looks at* SIR GEOFFREY; *sighs*). No; they hung him.

SIR G. (*laughs*). I am afraid I can't recommend you to my friends.

DALE (*seriously*). If the bad feeling between two friends of ours gets much worse, I think one of them will need legal advice. (*Comes down* C.)

SIR G. (*goes toward* DALE; *seriously*). Dale, do you really think there is danger of anything serious happening?

DALE. I do, indeed.

SIR G. (*as if meditating*). It is sad to contemplate. Two life-long friends at swords' points, because of their rivalry for a woman's love.

DALE (*spouting*). Love, love, what is love? It is the axis on which the world revolves; and as it goes around and around, over and over (*makes motions with hands*), is it any wonder that friends and friendships are turned topsy-turvy? O woman, if St. Peter is obliged to keep account of all the sins that can be laid at your door, what an army of clerks he must employ.

SIR G. (*impatiently*). Dale, do be serious for just a moment. I am really concerned for our friends. They go about looking daggers at each other.

DALE (*laughs*). Yes; and imagine no one sees them. Because love is blind, they fancy we are all afflicted with the same weakness.

SIR G. There you go again. I tell you, Dale, Miss Vaughn is likely to cause serious trouble between Roy and Captain Wyndham.

DALE (*seriously*). I quite agree with you; and the worst feature of the whole deplorable affair is that I don't think she is worth the trouble she is making.

SIR G. (*surprised*). Why, Dale! What do you mean?

DALE (*looks at* SIR GEOFFREY *a moment, before speaking*). Sir Geoffrey, I can speak plainly to you?

SIR G. Certainly, this is not gossip. It is our duty to discuss the matter, and, if possible, find a remedy. Go on, Dale.

DALE (*slowly*). Miss Vaughn really loves Captain Wyndham.

SIR G. Then how do you account for the many little favors she bestows upon Roy?

DALE (*slowly and impressively*). I said she *really* loved Captain Wyndham. But Captain Wyndham is poor. Miss Vaughn has expensive tastes which Wyndham could not indulge. (*Looks at* SIR GEOFFREY *meaningly.*) Now, Roy Darrell is rich.

SIR G. And you think —?

[*READY* JURA, *to enter* R. 3 E.

DALE (*in a brisk, business tone*). That Miss Vaughn will put her love away on a shelf until after her marriage with Roy; then she will take it down, carefully dust and brighten it up, and restore it to its former place.

SIR G. (*shocked*). Good Heavens, Dale, what are you saying?

DALE (*firmly*). What I believe to be the truth.

SIR G. Armstrong Dale, this is slander; I will not listen to it. (*Shoulders his gun.*)

DALE. Now, just a moment.

SIR G. (*sternly*). Not another word on this subject, as you value my friendship. (*EXIT*, L. 1 E.)

[*READY* ROY *and* WYNDHAM, *to enter* R. 1 E.

DALE (*looking after him*). That is always the way. A man asks you for the truth, but when you knock him down with it he carefully nurses the sore spot, and declares you struck him a foul blow. Moral: tell the truth, and you are voted a boor; lie, and you are hailed as a good fellow. (*Shoulders gun.*) I am done with the truth. (*Crosses over to* L.) Henceforth, I am a liar. (*EXIT*, L. 1 E.)

ENTER JURA, R. 3 E., *dressed roughly; he comes down* C., *looking after* DALE *and* SIR GEOFFREY.

JURA. So! it has become so plain that every fool staying at the castle gossips of it? Bah! Love! To let a silly, romantic love stand in the way of riches, a life of luxury! I have reasoned with her. Reason? How like an idiot I talk — as if you could reason with a woman. No, she will go on until she loses the prize. Loses it to gain — what? Captain Lionel Wyndham, gentleman. Bah — an aristocratic pauper! How I wish he were dead and out of her way — then she would come to her senses and marry Roy Darrell. With a bank account like that to draw upon (*snaps his fingers*), I could look Dame Fortune in the face, and laugh to think how some fools woo her.

[ROY *and* WYNDHAM *are heard off* R., *talking, gradually drawing nearer.*

(*Looks* R.) Some one coming! (*Looks* R. *again.*) Roy Darrell and — Captain Wyndham! (*Doubles up his fist, looks* R. *as if he would like to stay and meet* WYNDHAM *in a fight, then quickly retires* R. 2 E.)

ENTER WYNDHAM, R. I E., *followed by* ROY. *Both angry.*

WYNDHAM. I will not answer you. (*Walking across to* L.)
ROY (C., *sternly*). You must.
WYND. (*stops* L. C.; *in surprise*). Must?
ROY. You have hinted certain things; now you must make your meaning clear.
WYND. What do you want to know?
ROY. When and where did you meet Miss Vaughn?
WYND. (*unwillingly*). In London, two years ago.
ROY. Did you ever propose marriage to her?
WYND. (*same tone*). No.
ROY. Did any attachment exist between you?
WYND. (*same tone*). I decline to answer.
ROY (*angrily*). By Heaven, you shall!
WYND. (*same tone*). I shall not.
ROY (*in a great passion*). Then you shall ask my pardon for the insinuations you have cast upon her name, and you shall also ask the pardon of the lady who is to become my wife.
WYND. Your wife?
ROY. You heard me rightly. If Miss Vaughn will honor me by accepting my hand, I shall marry her before the month is out.
WYND. (*hotly*). You will do nothing of the kind.
ROY. And who will prevent it?
WYND. I will. (*Speaks quickly.*) We have been life-long friends. It is true some bad feeling has existed between us since you attempted to gain what I possessed, Viola's affections. But I did not dream that you thought of making her your wife. Now that I know your intentions, I shall interpose my friendship to prevent you from linking the proud name of Darrell to one that can only bring dishonor. [*READY* ALICE, *to enter* L. I E.
ROY (*with suppressed rage*). Make your meaning clear!
WYND. (*quietly*). Viola Vaughn is not a good woman.
ROY. Prove the truth of your words, or I will kill you.

WYND. I shall ride to the barracks this evening; to-morrow, at ten, I will meet you with the proofs that Viola Vaughn is my mistress.

ROY (*hotly*). You lie!

[*READY* DALE *and* SIR GEOFFREY, *to enter* L. 1 E.

WYND. What!

> [*Strikes* ROY, *who staggers back toward* R.; *he has a gun in his hands, right hand on stock, left hand on barrel; it is pointed at* WYNDHAM. JURA *comes out from* R. 2 E., *behind* ROY; *he reaches around him and pulls trigger of gun;* WYNDHAM *screams and falls* L. C. ROY *falls* R., *as if stunned by* WYNDHAM'S *blow.* NOTE: *A loop of wire should be attached to trigger of gun, so that* JURA *can easily get hold of it.*

ENTER ALICE, *with small basket,* L. 1 E. *She stands* L. *as shot is fired; she appears dazed.*

JURA (*crosses to* C., *and stands bending over* WYNDHAM). Curse you, I'm glad you are out of the way.

> [ALICE *screams, and drops basket.* JURA *looks up surprised.* ALICE *faints and falls* L. *This business is important, as it is repeated in Act III.*

(*Crosses quickly to* ALICE.) Fainted? Good! She was so frightened she won't remember me. (*Crosses to* WYNDHAM, *kneels and feels his heart.*) Dead. Now, Roy Darrell is free for Viola, and his bank account is open to me. (*Looking at* WYNDHAM.) What a fool Viola was ever to mix with you. (*Laughs.*) Well, you won't show your proofs to Lord Darrell — I blocked that little game. (*Noise* L., *as if people were approaching.*) Hark, some one is coming. I'm off. (*EXIT,* R. 1 E.)

DALE (*outside* L. 1 E.). This way, Sir Geoffrey.

ENTER DALE, L. 1 E. *He perceives* WYNDHAM, *goes to him, feels heart, etc. ENTER* SIR GEOFFREY, L. 1 E. *Sees* DALE *bending over* WYNDHAM.

SIR GEOFFREY (L.). What is it?

DALE. Murder! (*Sees* ROY *reviving,* R.) And Roy Darrell! (*Goes to* ROY, *gives him a drink from pocket-flask; examines* ROY.) He isn't hurt, only stunned.

SIR G. (*coming* C., *toward* DALE). How do you account for the woman's scream?

DALE (*who has been looking about, sees* ALICE). Here! (*Goes to* ALICE.) She has fainted. (*Gives her drink from flask.*)

> [ROY *attempts to rise;* SIR GEOFFREY *goes to* ROY *and assists him.*

SIR G. Darrell! Roy! Come, rouse yourself. (*Shakes him.*) What has happened?

ROY (*struggles to one knee; confused*). I can't say exactly — we quarrelled — Wyndham struck me — and —

Sir G. (c.). You shot him!

Roy (r. c.; *struggles to his feet*). Shot him? No, no!

Sir G. He is lying here, dead.

Roy. Dead? There is some mistake; I have no recollection of firing.

Dale (l. c.). Perhaps the girl can throw some light upon the mystery. (*Assists* Alice *to her feet.*) Are you better?

Alice (l.; *faintly*). Yes, thank you.

Dale. Can you tell us what you saw just before you fainted?

> [Alice *suddenly looks around; sees* Wyndham *lying there; recollects; covers her face with her hands, and shudders.*

Sir G. Come, my good girl, be brave; tell us what you saw.

Alice (*faintly*). I saw two men struggling; I saw a flash; both men fell; then — then I must have fainted.

Roy. But who fired the shot?

Alice (*looks at him*). The gun was in your hands.

Roy. Was there no one else here?

Alice. No — no one — yes, yes there was.

> [*Exclamation from all.*

Dale. Think, try to remember.

Alice (*slowly*). I can just remember a dark man with an evil face — he seemed to be standing behind this gentleman when he fell. I can't remember anything more.

Dale. Would you know this man if you were to see him again?

Alice. I think I should.

Dale (*with decision*). We must find that man.

Sir G. Yes, but in the meantime Darrell may be convicted and hanged.

Roy. Hanged! Merciful heaven! You are not in earnest — a Darrell hanged! O mother, mother, it would kill her. (*Fiercely.*) They shall not hang me.

Sir G. The case is very black. I can think of no way to save you.

Dale (*suddenly*). But I can. This girl is the only witness to the crime, except the man who ran away. In England, a wife cannot be compelled to give evidence against her husband. Darrell, if this girl will become your wife, they cannot convict you.

> [*General movement of astonishment.*

Sir G. Think what you are proposing!

Dale. I am proposing a means to gain time to find this man. It is your only hope, Darrell — decide quickly.

Roy (*crosses in front of* Sir Geoffrey, *to* c. Sir Geoffrey *drops down* r.; *to* Alice). Will you consent? Think before you speak. It is not to save my life that I ask you to do this. It is for my dear mother's sake. I am all she has in the world to love and lean upon. (*Holds out his hand to* Alice, *who comes slowly* c. Dale *drops down* l.) She is getting old, and needs my care. If

I were taken away to imprisonment or death, it would kill her. Think of my mother, and give me your answer.

ALICE (*slowly*). I consent. (*Gives her hand to* ROY, *who shakes it as if thanking her.*)

DALE. We must be quick. (*Looks off,* L. I E.) Officers are searching the wood. (*To* SIR GEOFFREY.) Sir Geoffrey, you are a magistrate, perform the shortest marriage ceremony that is legal.

SIR G. (*expostulating*). But a marriage without a license is not legal in England. Besides, I am a Scotch magistrate. The marriage is impossible.

[*READY* DALTON, *to enter* L. I. E.

DALE (*thinks a moment*). Hold on. Roy, look about you. (ROY *does so.*) Tell me, isn't this part of your estate on Scottish soil?

ROY (*looks*). Yes; just over the English border.

DALE (*briskly*). All right, Sir Magistrate; go ahead. (*Takes out watch; holds it in hand.*)

SIR. G. (*goes up stage behind* ROY *and* ALICE; *to* ROY *and* ALICE). Join hands. (*They do so.*) Roy Darrell, do you take this woman (*to* ALICE) — what is your name?

ALICE. Alice Paisey.

SIR G. Alice Paisey, for your wife?

ROY. I do.

SIR G. Alice Paisey, do you take this man, Roy Darrell, for your husband?

ALICE. I do.

SIR G. With the authority vested me as a magistrate, I pronounce you man and wife. [ALICE *and* ROY *drop down to* R. C.

DALE. Hurrah, one minute and thirty-two seconds — the quickest on record. I'll bet it would take a good deal longer to undo it.

ENTER DALTON, L. I E.

WYNDHAM C.

SIR GEOFFREY.   DALE.

ALICE.

ROY.   DALTON L.

R. ROY'S *gun.*

DALTON. Ah, good-evening to you, gentlemen. One of my men heard a shot and a woman's scream. We've been searching, but haven't found anything yet. (*Notices that they look strange.*) Nothing wrong, I hope?

SIR G. Yes; there is something wrong. (*Steps toward* DALE; *they both step aside to* L., *disclosing body of* WYNDHAM.)

DALTON (*goes quickly to* WYNDHAM; *feels his heart*). Dead! Shot! (*Crosses to* ROY'S *gun, picks it up and looks at it.*) Your gun, Lord Darrell?

ROY (R. C.). Yes.

DALTON (R.). I must place you under arrest. (*To* DALE *and*

SIR GEOFFREY.)   Were either of you gentlemen here when this happened?

SIR G. (L. C.).   No.   [DALE, L., *shakes his head negatively.*

DALTON (*to* ALICE).   Were you here?

ALICE (C., *slowly*).   Yes.

DALTON.   Ah, a witness!   Who fired the shot?

ALICE (*firmly*).   I decline to answer.

DALTON (*in surprise*).   Decline to answer!   You must.   A crime has been committed; you are shielding the criminal; I shall arrest you as an accomplice; and the law will compel you to speak. Now, answer.

ALICE.   I refuse.   You may arrest me, you may throw me into prison, but I shall not answer.   The law is powerless to compel me, for I am Lord Darrell's wife!

[DALTON astonished; DALE triumphant.

PICTURE.

WYNDHAM, C.

ALICE.

ROY.   DALE.

R.   DALTON.   SIR GEOFFREY.   L.

CURTAIN.

ACT II.

SCENE. — The home of LORD DARRELL; *a handsome interior. For description of setting, see scene-plot. ENTER* VIOLA, *c., just after rise, as the clock is striking. She stops and listens. The clock strikes seven.*

VIOLA (*up* C.). Seven o'clock! he may be here at any moment. (*Comes down* L.) But for her, how changed it would be! How blind I was! how Lionel wove the veil around my eyes — fool that I was to believe him, and lose my chance with Roy. (*Meditating.*) Roy did love me once; but does he still? (*Leans on piano.*) He has been away four months. Four months are not a lifetime, but many changes can take place in that time. (*Looks in glass; arranges hair; laughs softly to herself.*) We shall see. As for my Lady Alice (*looks at herself again in mirror*), I flatter myself she will be no great rival.

ENTER LADY DARRELL, C.

LADY DARRELL (*sees* VIOLA; *goes toward her*). Ah, Viola, you look charming this evening. (*Kisses her on forehead.*) I have not heard wheels on the gravel; it is growing late, and he has not come.

VIOLA. You are over-anxious, dear. (*Leads* LADY DARRELL *to seat at table; she stands* L., *and behind chair.*) By the way, does Roy bring any one with him? I think I heard you say something about guests.

LADY D. Yes; he will be accompanied by a gentleman that he met in Italy — a Count Jura; and, from Roy's letters, a most delightful companion. I am glad that Roy is bringing him; otherwise life here might prove too trying for you.

VIOLA. Not at all, dear; I haven't found it dull. I have you to converse with; and when I have nothing else to do, I amuse myself with the Countess. By-the-by, did I understand you to say she was to come to the drawing-room to-night?

LADY D. (*frowns*). Yes; I insisted that she should not shut herself up in her rooms, but meet her husband on his home-coming in her proper place and position. We shall have guests to-night, and cannot risk scandal by her absence. But I tremble for her conduct and behavior.

VIOLA. Let us hope she will not commit any flagrant breach of good manners. (*Sneeringly.*) I dare say, with her country bows and manners, she will be quite amusing.

ENTER ALICE C., *in time to hear the last of* VIOLA'S *speech. She is dressed elegantly, and is dignified in manner. Comes slowly down* R.

ALICE. I shall be glad to afford Miss Vaughn amusement. (*To* LADY DARRELL.) Good-evening, Lady Darrell.
   [LADY DARRELL *and* VIOLA *look at* ALICE *in surprise, on account of her superb and easy manner.*

LADY D. (*bows haughtily*). Welcome, Countess; will you not sit down?   [ALICE *crosses and sits on sofa,* C.) (*Aside.*) Where does she get her patrician air? (*Crosses to* ALICE; *impulsively.*) Have you any recollection of your childhood? Did you always live with your aunt? Which side are your relations?
   [VIOLA *crosses down* L., *looking at* LADY DARRELL, *interested.*

ALICE, C.

LADY DARRELL, L. C. VIOLA, L.

ALICE (*surprised*). I can remember nothing clearly. I have a dim recollection of a large house, and of a beautiful face bending over me. Then came long years with Aunt Martha, and all her angry words.

VIOLA (*sneeringly*). What a pity you cannot remember clearly — we might have discovered a secret, or a long-lost father. You might have developed into a queen. As it is —

ALICE (*interrupting quietly*). As it is, I am only Alice — Alice, the farm-girl.

LADY D. (*frowns*). Roy is late; I will go to my room until he arrives. (*Bows haughtily to* ALICE, *smiles at* VIOLA, *crosses behind sofa, and EXIT* R. 3 E.)

ALICE (*aside*). I must not tell them anything of what Aunt Martha said about my mother; it might bring shame upon her memory.   .

VIOLA (*to* ALICE, *banteringly*). My lady Alice, it is an unexpected pleasure to see you in the drawing-room. I wonder you were persuaded to leave your dearly loved books. What a store of learning my lord will find in his wife's head when he returns. By the way, have you heard from those worthy people, your aunt and uncle, since they left the village?

ALICE. No.   [*READY* SIR GEOFFREY *to enter* C.

VIOLA. They are not very considerate of their niece's welfare.

ALICE. Aunt Martha is only too glad to be rid of me; she always looked upon me as a burden, and —

VIOLA. And glad to see you happily and well married? (*Smiles.*) I suppose it was natural. Did Lord Darrell mention the name of the gentleman he is bringing home with him?

ALICE. I did not know he was to bring a gentleman with him; he has not written to me.

VIOLA (*sneeringly*). Not written to you? Ah, that was remiss! I suppose he was busy, and forgot to write; probably he intends it as a surprise, for he didn't mention his name in the letter I received this morning. (*Goes up stage; looks off* C. *to* L.)

ALICE (*rises and goes down* R.; *chokingly*). He wrote to her — not a line to me! Oh, I will go away! (*Regains command of herself.*) No; I shall not let her triumph over me.

[*READY* DALE, *to enter* C.

VIOLA. Ah, here is Sir Geoffrey!

ENTER SIR GEOFFREY, C.

SIR GEOFFREY. Good-evening, Miss Vaughn. (VIOLA *bows; he sees* ALICE.) And Countess! (*Comes down stage to* ALICE; *shakes hands with her.* VIOLA *comes down* L.) This is an unexpected pleasure. Are you feeling quite well? (*Is looking at her intently.*)

ALICE (R.). Quite well, Sir Geoffrey, thank you.

SIR G. (C.). Do you know, Countess, you remind me greatly of some one I knew years ago?

ALICE (*with interest*). Indeed! May I ask whom?

SIR G. (*thoughtfully*). That is what puzzles me; I don't know.

VIOLA (*down* L.). Again? Try to remember, Sir Geoffrey; we may yet find that our countess has the blue blood of nobility.

SIR G. (*rather sharply*). My dear Miss Vaughn, I have known men and women in whose veins coursed the bluest blood, who were the most degenerate. No; purity of mind, goodness of heart, are the attributes which make true nobility.

ENTER DALE, C., *in time to hear the last of* SIR GEOFFREY'S *speech.*

DALE. Quite right, Sir Geoffrey. (*Comes down* R. *of sofa, between* VIOLA *and* SIR GEOFFREY.) That's what makes me a nobleman in all but name. Good-evening, Miss Vaughn. (*Bus. to* VIOLA.) Countess. I'm charmed to see you again. (*Crosses* R. *and shakes hands with* ALICE.)

[SIR GEOFFREY *crosses and talks with* VIOLA.

ALICE, R.   DALE, C.   SIR G., L. C.   VIOLA, L.

ALICE (*smiling*).   Mr. Dale, you always bring sunshine and laughter with you.   I am glad you've come.

DALE (*airily*).   My dear Countess, that is my greeting every-where.   I have the reputation of being an amusing fellow, a funny man.   [SIR GEOFFREY *and* VIOLA *retire up, in conversation.*

ALICE.   I am sure you should feel pleased.

DALE.   I would if I had time.

ALICE.   Had time !   Why, I fail to catch your meaning.

DALE.   Being a funny man, I am in demand.   Should a friend be giving a dinner at which all the old maids and old fogies for miles around are to be present, the host, with a happy thought, says, " I will invite Dale ; he will keep us all in good humor."   If there is a wedding, a christening, a lawn-party, a boating or riding-party, I am invited ; not because they *want* me — oh, dear, no ; but just to be funny.   In fact, I am wanted everywhere but at funerals, all because of my reputation of being funny.   I have to sit up half the night, and frequently lock myself in all day, think-ing up amusing things to say.

                         [*READY* ROY *and* JURA, *to enter* C.

ALICE.   That's very good of you ; and I am sure your friends appreciate it.

DALE.   No, they don't ; they seem to think it is natural for me to be funny.   They won't take me seriously.   I find it a great drawback to advancement in my profession.   Why, a few days since, I argued a case for a poor woman whose husband had been hurt by an omnibus ; several of my acquaintances were on the jury ; I prepared a most touching appeal.   Did they take it seri-ously ?   Did they weep, as I expected ?   No, they laughed — laughed until tears ran down their cheeks ; they insisted that I was funny.   I lost the case, and was reprimanded by the judge for provoking levity in the court.

ALICE.   I sympathize with you, and promise not to laugh at anything you say this evening ; so for once you can be serious. (*Gives him her hand.*)

DALE (*with mock effusion*).   Thank you, Countess.   You have applied the salve of sympathy to my wounded feelings.   (*Has his hand on his heart.*)

VIOLA (*up* R. C.).   Hark !   Isn't that the carriage ?

SIR G. (*up* R. C., *looking toward* C. *door*).   Yes, you are right ; they have arrived.

ROY (*outside*).   James, look after the luggage ; we will go at once to the drawing-room.

                         [ALICE *trembles at the sound of* ROY'S *voice.*

DALE.   Countess, are you ill ?

ALICE.   It is nothing ; I am a little dizzy, that is all.   I shall be myself in a moment. (*Takes a step or two toward* R. DALE *goes up* C., *above sofa.*)

ENTER ROY, C., *followed by* JURA.

ROY. Ah, Sir Geoffrey — and Dale (*shaking hands with them*); so good of you to be here to welcome me. Allow me to introduce Count Jura; Sir Geoffrey Rawdon, Mr. Armstrong Dale. (*The gentlemen shake hands.* ROY *crosses* L. *to* VIOLA; *eagerly.*) Viola — Miss Vaughn, I can't tell you how happy I am to renew our friendship. (*Takes her hand;* VIOLA *indicates* ALICE; ROY *turns and sees her; bows coldly.*) I hope I see you well, Countess?

DALE.
JURA.   SIR G.
[SOFA.]

R., ALICE.   ROY. VIOLA, L.

ALICE (*quietly*). Quite well, my lord.

JURA (*to* ROY; *looking at* ALICE *with admiration*). My lord, I beg the honor of meeting the countess.

[*READY* LADY DARRELL, *to enter* R. 3 E.

ROY. I beg your pardon, Count Jura; allow me to present you to my — (*hesitates*) — wife.

JURA (*crosses to* ALICE, *and takes her hand*). Countess, I am charmed to meet you. (*Kisses her hand.* ALICE *draws away her hand.*)

ALICE. Thank you. [JURA *looks at her; she shrinks away.*

ROY. My dear Jura (JURA *turns toward* L.), let me introduce you to my guest, Miss Vaughn.

·   [VIOLA *looks at* JURA *for the first time, and starts in terror.* JURA *crosses* L. *to* VIOLA. ROY *drops down* C.

JURA. Miss Vaughn, delighted. (*Bows to* VIOLA, *and smiles at her mockingly.*)   [VIOLA *bows silently.*

ENTER LADY DARRELL, R. 3 E. *She crosses quickly to* ROY.

LADY D. Roy, my son!

ROY (*embracing her*). Mother! Count Jura, let me present you to my mother, Lady Darrell.

DALE. SIR G.
[SOFA.] LADY D.
ROY.
JURA.

R., ALICE.   VIOLA, L.

JURA (*bows*). I feel as if I already knew Lady Darrell, from my many conversations with her noble son.

> [LADY DARRELL *bows; speaks aside to* ROY.

VIOLA (*aside to* JURA). I must see you alone. Meet me here in a few moments.   [JURA *nods assent.*

ALICE (*aside, looking intently at* JURA). Where have I seen that man before?

ROY. Let us go into the conservatory. I am sure we shall find it cool and pleasant there. Sir Geoffrey, give your arm to Lady Darrell.

> [SIR GEOFFREY *gives* LADY DARRELL *his arm; they
> cross and EXEUNT,* L. 1 E.

Dale, will you give your arm to the Countess?

> [DALE *comes down* R. *of* ALICE. ROY *takes* VIOLA'S
> *arm and EXIT with her,* L. 1 E.

JURA (*quickly crosses to* ALICE, *and offers his arm*). Allow me.

> [ALICE *hesitates; then takes his arm. They cross and
> EXEUNT,* L. 1 E.

DALE (*looking after them angrily*). Cut out by that confounded foreigner! Who in the deuce is he, anyway? He is a count; he has that magic title tacked to his name, that dazzles the eyes of all women. I'll go after them. (*Starts a step or two toward* L.) What, and see him gloat over the countess, of whom he has taken possession? No; I'll turn to man's comfort, that always remains to him. (*Up to* C. D.) I'll go into the garden and smoke a cigar. (*EXIT,* C.)

ENTER ALICE, *hurriedly,* L. 1 E.

ALICE. I slipped away from them. I can't endure this. He loves her, and I came between them; but for me she would have been his wife. Oh, I am unhappy, miserable! (*Crosses during speech to* R., *and sinks into chair behind screen.*)

ENTER VIOLA *quickly,* L. 1 E. *She looks about, but does not see* ALICE.

VIOLA. I must speak to this Count Jura at once. Did he notice me leave the conservatory? (*Looks off,* L.) Yes; he is coming.

ENTER JURA, L. 1 E.

JURA (*to* VIOLA). Well?

> [ALICE *starts at the sound of his voice; she cannot help
> hearing their conversation.*

VIOLA (L. C.; *imperiously*). Why did you come here?

JURA (L.; *laughs*). Why did you come?

VIOLA. That is not an answer to my question. I am an invited guest here.

JURA (*lightly*). So am I.

VIOLA. How came you to be invited?

JURA (*matter-of-fact tone*). I met Lord Darrell in Italy, where I was masquerading as a count; he invited me to his home; I accepted.

VIOLA (*angrily*). Again I ask, why did you come?

JURA (*laughs banteringly*). To be near my dear sister. I am your only living relative; it is but natural I should wish to be near you.

VIOLA. You must leave here. There is too great danger that this imposture be discovered. Should the London police get upon your track, should it become known that you are my brother, what would these people think?

JURA. You mean, what would Roy Darrell think? (*Angrily.*) Why didn't you grasp Lord Darrell when you had the chance? What fool's nonsense was in your head?

VIOLA (*sadly*). Love.

JURA. Love? (*Laughs.*) No, no. sister mine; to lose a title and a fortune for love? Some other tale, please.

VIOLA. It is the truth. I loved Lionel Wyndham. You did not see — you were blind to what was going on in our little cottage at Hampden, when Lionel's regiment was quartered close by.

JURA (*threateningly*). If I had known it, it would have ended long before it did.

VIOLA. When I came to the castle. you thought I did so to please you. It was to follow Lionel. I had grown jealous. He was changing toward me. Lady Darrell had often written to press me for a visit, so I embraced the opportunity. Roy did exactly as you prophesied, — fell in love with me at once. I cared only for Lionel. A coolness arose between the two men over me. The day before the murder, Roy came to me and begged for my love. I accepted him. resolving to be a fool no longer. Then came the murder — his marriage — and he was lost to me forever.

[*READY* ROY, *to enter* L. 1 E.

JURA. Forever? (*Slowly.*) That is a long time, Viola. I do not think you need wait that long.

VIOLA. Don't be absurd; do you forget that he has a wife?

JURA (*slowly*). No; but if you play your cards right, I fancy *he* will forget it before long.

VIOLA. Leave me to play my cards; but if you wish me to win, leave here at once. Go, go!

JURA (*mockingly*). Now that is sisterly affection! No. my dear: my visit has a purpose. Until it is accomplished. I remain.

VIOLA.   What is your purpose?

JURA (*laughs*).   Inquisitive woman! Later, sister mine, you shall know. (*Takes her arm, and they EXEUNT C., talking.*)

ALICE (*staggers from behind screen*).   Am I dreaming? Her brother! Police! Let me think. (*Presses hand to forehead.*) Shall I tell my husband of this?   [*Laughter heard off* L. 1 E. No; he would call it a silly fancy, and I should be laughed at. (*Stands dejectedly* R., *with her back toward* L.)

ENTER ROY, L. 1 E., *with bouquet. He mistakes* ALICE *for* VIOLA, *and crosses to her.*

ROY (*in a low, eager tone*).   Viola, I have kept my promise; here are your flowers.   [ALICE *turns.* (*Taken aback.*) Lady Darrell — you! (*Is suddenly struck with her appearance.*) How beautiful you are!

ALICE (*simply*).   Thank you; I trust I am to your satisfaction. If you wish to find Miss Vaughn, she just stepped out on the balcony.

ROY (*confused*).   I brought her· some flowers; she always likes them.

ALICE (*noticing his confusion*).   Flowers such as these are worth liking. I never saw so many wonderful plants until I came here.

ROY (*looking intently at her*).   Our hot-houses are considered very fine. We must go over them together.

ALICE.   I am afraid it would be too much trouble, my lord.
                    [*READY* VIOLA *and* JURA *to enter* C.
ROY.   Trouble? Oh, no! I had almost forgotten; my mother wishes you to wear the Darrell diamonds to-night. See, I have brought them to you. (*Opens cases he has in hand; shows diamonds.*)

[*READY* LADY DARRELL *and* SIR GEOFFREY *to enter* L. 1 E.
ALICE (*impulsively*).   How lovely!

ROY.   Now put them on; I will assist you. (*They get toward* C. *He puts necklace and diadem on her, as* ALICE *puts on rings, etc. He stands off and surveys her.*) Now, tell me at what hour you will be free to-morrow, and I shall be at your service.

ALICE.   I am free all day.

ROY (*taking her hand*).   Then we can —

ENTER VIOLA, C., *followed by* JURA. *She takes in the situation at a glance, and frowns.*

VIOLA.   Ah, Lord Darrell, I have been looking for you. (*Comes down* L. C., *between* ALICE *and* ROY. JURA *comes down* R. *of* ALICE.)

R., JURA.   ALICE, C.   VIOLA, L. C.   ROY, L.

ALICE. I am trying to console my husband, Miss Vaughn; he was seeking you disconsolately with his promised gift of flowers. (*Crosses to* JURA, *who has been watching her intently.*)

> [ROY *watches them, and gives flowers mechanically to*
> VIOLA. *READY* DALE, *to enter* C.

ENTER LADY DARRELL *and* SIR GEOFFREY, L. I E.

VIOLA (*to* ROY). This is very kind of you.

ROY (*looking abstractedly at* ALICE). Oh, no; not at all. I promised them.   [*They go up stage, and talk apart.*

LADY DARRELL (*to* SIR GEOFFREY, *looking at* ALICE, *who is talking apart to* JURA, R.). Where does she get her manner? She is a patrician from head to foot.

JURA (*to* ALICE). Countess, you are divine, superb! These old halls have seen no one to compare with you, my Lady Darrell.

ALICE. You flatter me, Count.

JURA. Flatter you? Ah, my Lady Darrell, you judge me harshly. I never saw life or happiness until I beheld you.

ALICE (*uneasily*). You are attracted by the diamonds, not me.

JURA. Diamonds? (*Notices diamonds for the first time.*) So you wear the celebrated Darrell gems to-night. Countess, you would be good booty for a robber.

ENTER DALE, C. *He speaks to* ROY *and* VIOLA *a moment, then drops down* C., *behind sofa.*

ALICE (*laughs*). But I am not afraid of robbers.

JURA. Women are always brave. Now, I am a man, but I don't mind confessing that I should not care to sleep in a room with those world-famous jewels.

ALICE. I have never tried it. I shall do so to-night for the first time. I will let you know to-morrow whether my slumbers are disturbed.

DALE (*crosses to* ALICE). Lady Darrell, this is unfair. You haven't given me a five-minute chat this evening.

ALICE (*laughing*). To-night is my first experience of this kind; usually I could give you hours. (*With a sigh.*) I suppose to-morrow I sha'n't have a soul to speak to.

DALE (*quickly*). Then mark my name down on your engagement list; I shall call after breakfast and occupy your whole day.

ALICE (*laughs*). I am sure you will be welcome. (*They go up the stage, talking.*)

> [ROY *and* VIOLA *come down.* ROY *crosses to* LADY
> DARRELL *and* SIR GEOFFREY. VIOLA *stands* C.,
> *looking at* JURA *a moment. Then she looks at* ROY
> *and* LADY DARRELL.

JURA (R., *aside*). To-night! To-night! To-night, she said.
It is well. (*Looking at* ALICE.) How beautiful she is! What
are diamonds to such loveliness? If I could clasp her in my arms,
and press my lips to hers —! Pshaw, I'm raving; it can never
be. George, old fellow, wake up! Remember, you have work
to-night. (*Stands* R., *looking at* ALICE.)

LADY D. (*to* ROY, *looking at* ALICE). Roy, she does well to-
night. How beautiful she is!

ROY (*to his mother*). Thank you, dearest; she is, indeed, most
beautiful. Mother, I begin to think we have judged her harshly.
Recollect, she married me to save my life.　　　[JURA *goes up* R.

LADY D. I do remember it, and in the future she shall be
welcome to me as my daughter. My pride has been against her
all this time, but to-night she stands revealed a lady. You have
no reason to blush for your wife.

ROY. I shall see the Paiseys, and make every inquiry about
her birth. I am certain she has proud blood in her veins, and
does not belong to them.

VIOLA (*who has been listening*). Discussing my Lady Darrell?
She has really astonished me. What a born actress the girl is!

ROY (*coldly*). Actress? It is not acting, Miss Vaughn; it is
nature.

VIOLA (*changing her tone*). I congratulate you; it has been a
severe test, and no one among your friends is more pleased at her
success than I am.

ROY (*warmly*). Thank you, Viola; it is like you to be so
kind. I am anxious that you should be friends with my — my —
the countess. You are so clever; you can help her.

VIOLA. My Lady Darrell does not need my aid. But, Roy,
since *you* wish it, I will be her friend for your sake.

ROY (*takes* VIOLA'S *hand for a moment; to* LADY DARRELL
and VIOLA). Excuse me. (*Crosses to* ALICE, *who is coming
down stage with* DALE, VIOLA *watching them.*)

SIR GEOFFREY (*offers* LADY DARRELL *his arm; they start* L.,
then stop). I am afraid Roy's request was rather ill-timed.

　　　　　　　DALE.　　ALICE.　　ROY.
　　　　　　　　╲　[SOFA.]
　　　　　　　　　　VIOLA.
R., JURA.　　　　　　　　　LADY DARRELL.
　　　　　　　　　　　　SIR GEOFFREY, L.

LADY D. What request?

SIR G. Asking Miss Vaughn to be his wife's friend.

LADY D. You are right. Viola will never be her friend.
Roy should not have asked her. But he is like all men — clumsy.

SIR G. Now, that is slandering the poor men; I protest. (*EXIT* L. I E., *with* LADY DARRELL, *laughing and expostulating.*)

ROY (*to* ALICE).   Will you walk as far as the conservatory? I will get you an ice.

DALE (*mock-tragically*).   I have Lady Darrell's promise to eat ices with no one but me.

ROY (*laughing*).   Remember, I am this lady's husband, and for the first time I exercise my authority, and command her to obey me.

ALICE (*laughing*).   I yield.   (*Takes* ROY'S *arm; they start* L.)

DALE (*calling after them*).   I have always heard that husbands were brutes; now I believe it.

ROY (*crossing in front of* VIOLA. L.).   Come, Jura. Miss Vaughn, won't you join us?

VIOLA.   Thank you, presently.

[*EXEUNT* ROY *and* ALICE, L. I E., VIOLA *looking after them.*

DALE (*coming down* C.; *to* VIOLA).   Don't you think the countess charming?

VIOLA (L.).   That is a matter of taste; she seems to have turned all of your heads.   Have you all lost your senses?

DALE.   We should certainly have lost our sense of the beautiful if we did not appreciate the loveliness of the countess.

VIOLA (*sneeringly*).   Lord Darrell had best be careful; with such an ardent admirer of his wife's in the house, he may lose Lady Darrell.

DALE (*indignantly*).   Lord Darrell is my friend. I am his guest. A gentleman never forgets the respect due the wife of his host. I wish I could say as much for the lady guests.

VIOLA.   You are insolent.

DALE.   I mentioned no names.

VIOLA.   I suppose that is a specimen of your cheap wit. I fail to find it amusing; try again, when I am in better humor.

DALE.   I am afraid my cheap wit will never find favor with you. I think tragedy is more in your line.

VIOLA.   Really, you are dense.   I have always given you credit for good sense, but if you continue in this way, I must doubt your sanity.

DALE.   But you can never doubt my intentions.   (*Crosses* L.) Miss Vaughn, I was one of the first persons in this house who met Lady Alice.   While in the forest at the scene of the tragedy, I conceived a strong liking for her; I am proud to be numbered among her friends.   And as her friend, I shall always be in readiness to defend her or to come to her aid.   (*Bows to* VIOLA, *and EXIT* L. I E.)

VIOLA (*looking after* DALE). Fool! Oh, this girl with her baby face — if I could but crush her, could but disgrace her!

JURA (*approaches quietly ; beside* VIOLA). You can.

VIOLA (*turns quickly*). What do you say?

JURA. I say you can rid yourself of her forever, and at the same time make it possible for you to become Lady Darrell.

VIOLA. How? How?

JURA. Listen, sister mine. You know me too well to think that I am here merely for pleasure. No, no; it is business that brings me here.

VIOLA (*sneeringly*). Stealing?

JURA. Exactly. I am here after the Darrell diamonds.

VIOLA. Impossible!

JURA. Not so. Lady Darrell wears them to-night. What could be easier than that you should slip into her room under pretence of a good-night chat? A handkerchief, a little chloroform, and the diamonds are mine.

VIOLA. And you expect me to help you in your devilish work?

JURA. Certainly.

VIOLA. I will do nothing of the kind. I will not listen to anything more you have to say. I will join the others. (*Starts toward* L.)

JURA (*threateningly*). Oh, yes you will, when I show how you will be benefited.   [VIOLA *stops.*

VIOLA (*turns to him*). Well, how?

JURA (*laughs softly*). It is well known that Roy Darrell does not love his wife — that he has neglected her. He left home immediately after his marriage, and has just returned after four months' absence. During that time the countess has been little less than a prisoner in her own room. This is the first time she has appeared among the guests in this house. She meets a gentleman (*draws himself up*), a good-looking, pleasant, agreeable gentleman, who pays her marked attention. Suppose, to-morrow morning, Lady Darrell and that gentleman, together with the Darrell diamonds, should be missing, what conclusion would people naturally reach?

VIOLA (*quickly*). Elopement!

JURA. You have voiced the general opinion.

VIOLA (*doubtfully*). Roy may not believe it.

JURA. What! (*Insinuatingly.*) And you here to fit in the details?

VIOLA. But where will you take her? Roy would follow, to kill you for outraging his hospitality; and Dale — do not forget that he is a friend of Lady Darrell's who will be hard to escape.

JURA. Do not fear, sister mine; I have my plans all laid. You know the old abbey ruins? Under those ruins there are vaults whose existence I doubt even the owner of the abbey suspects. One of my pals, an old hag, and her daughter are there. To-night they will be in the grounds to help me if necessary. We can easily keep my lady under the influence of chloroform until we get her in the vaults; there we will stay for a few days while they search the country. Then I'll slip off to my den in London, and at the first opportunity we will sail for Italy.

[*READY* ROY *and* ALICE *to enter* L. I E.

VIOLA. How can you hope to subdue her so that she will yield to your plans?

JURA. Leave that to me. Once she is convinced that her husband and the rest of them think she is a thief — that she stole the diamonds and eloped with me — it will be easy enough. Come, will you aid me?

VIOLA (*thinks a moment*). Yes.

JURA. Good. Here is where I can be found in London. (*Writes on card.*) Should any danger threaten, don't write, but come. (*Gives* VIOLA *card; looks* L.) Here come Roy and Lady Darrell. You get Roy out of the way, and be sure to drop a few hints of the attentions I am paying his wife.

ENTER ROY *and* ALICE, L. I E.

(*Sauntering toward* R.) Yes, Miss Vaughn, I have seen many bull-fights in Spain. They are, indeed, exciting — don't you think so, Lord Darrell? [VIOLA, C.

ROY (L). No, I can't say that I do — I never attended but one, and to my mind it was brutal.

VIOLA (C). I quite agree with you, Lord Darrell.

JURA (R.; *to* ALICE). What is your opinion, Countess?

ALICE (*crosses* C., *to* JURA). I think the same as Miss Vaughn; it is inhuman to torture dumb brutes.

VIOLA (*aside to* ROY). Roy, I would like to talk with you a few moments. Will you take me into the garden?

ROY. Certainly. (*To* JURA *and* ALICE.) Excuse us Count — Lady Darrell?

[ALICE *and* JURA *bow;* ROY *and* VIOLA *EXEUNT*
C.; ALICE *starts towards* L.

JURA. Ah, Countess, don't leave me, come sit here, we can have a quiet little chat.

ALICE. Really, Count, I have my guests to attend to.

JURA. Am I not one? (ALICE *sits on sofa; aside.*) She is unhappy. I might win her without force; I'll try. (*Sits on sofa beside* ALICE; *aloud.*) So you think the Spaniards are cruel to indulge in bull-fights? Well, perhaps you are right. It is a beautiful country, but not so fair as Italy.

ALICE (*dreamily*).   I should be glad to travel and see other lands.

JURA.   You would?   How would you like to leave this cold, desolate place, and see nothing but blue sky, sunshine, and flowers?   Fancy a garden with orange-groves scenting the air, with terraces leading down to a bay as blue — as blue as your star-like eyes.   Ah, one can be happy in a home like that!

ALICE (*eagerly*).   Do you know of such a place?

JURA.   Yes, I know of such a paradise; it is mine — all mine. Now it stands empty and deserted; it only awaits a mistress — a mistress fair, lovely as the sun, with gentle grace and maddening eyes; eyes such as yours —

ALICE (*attempting to rise*).   Count —

JURA (*his arm around* ALICE'S *waist; passionately*).   Alice, you are the only woman in this wide world that could bring happiness in such a home.   Have not my eyes spoken clearly?   Did you not understand?   [ALICE *struggling to free herself.* Alice, my Lady Alice, listen.   I will take you away from all this gilded misery.   You are wretched here; I can give you all this, and love besides.   You cannot comprehend what a passion is devouring my heart; for you I live alone, for I love you!

        [*READY* ROY *and* VIOLA *to enter* C.

ALICE (*breaking away from him;* C.).   Let me go!   How dare you insult me like this!

JURA (*rises*).   Insult?   What! you pretend not to have seen my love?

ALICE.   Your love?   (*Scornfully.*)   I have seen nothing.   If I had, should I be here to be insulted?   Go: go at once; you are my husband's guest, but you betray the trust he reposes in you.   I scorn, I hate you!

        [*READY* DALE, LADY DARRELL, *and* SIR GEOFFREY *to enter* L. I E.

JURA (R. C.).   Beware, my Lady Darrell!   I am your friend — your lover — now; but make me your enemy, and I will fight you to the bitter end.

ALICE.   I am not frightened.   A man who threatens a woman is a coward.   Go!

JURA.   You shall sue to me yet; you shall be in my power.   I swear it!   (*Quickly puts his arm around* ALICE; *as he does so*)

VIOLA *and* ROY *ENTER* C.   VIOLA *points to* JURA *and* ALICE.

I love you, and I will not give you up!

        [ROY *comes down quickly*, L. *of* ALICE.   VIOLA *comes down* L. *of* ROY.

ROY (*to* ALICE, *in a rage*).   Lady Darrell, what is the meaning of this?

ALICE. It means that this man has betrayed your hospitality and insulted me.

JURA (*passionately*). It is a lie! You accepted my advances willingly.

ALICE. Lord Darrell, that you do not love me, I know. But if you respect the name I bear, you will resent this insult — you will strike that man! [ROY *crosses quickly, and knocks* JURA *down.*

ENTER DALE, LADY DARRELL, *and* SIR GEOFFREY, *quickly,*
L. 1 E.

PICTURE.
VIOLA.

ALICE.   DALE.

ROY.   LADY DARRELL.

R., JURA.   SIR GEOFFREY, L.

CURTAIN.

ACT III.

SCENE I. — *A room in* LORD DARRELL'S *house. Plain chamber in* 1*st groove. Doors* R. C. *and* L. C. *in the flat. READY* LADY DARRELL *to enter* R. C.

ROY (*speaks outside at rise of curtain*). James, have the horses saddled and ready in an hour. (*ENTER*, L. 1 E.) By Jove! I never felt better in my life. If it wasn't for the dark cloud of Captain Wyndham's death that hangs over me, I should say this is the happiest day of my life. How beautiful she was last night! No lady in the land could have been more superb. That scoundrel Jura, I should shoot him, but I shall rest content with branding him a scoundrel. He shall leave here to-day. How Alice's eyes flashed as she denounced him! There is blood in her veins as blue as flows in any Darrell, I am sure of it. I have left her all these months neglected, unhappy, despised; but now all shall be changed. How do I know she will forgive me? This morning I shall ask her pardon, and if she grants it, we will go to Italy or some other sunny place, where I will make amends for the past.

LADY DARRELL *knocks at door and ENTERS* R. C.

LADY DARRELL. Up so early, Roy?
ROY. Yes, mother. (*Kisses her.*) I am going for a ride.
LADY D. With your wife, eh? (*Looks at him laughingly.*)
ROY. Mother, you see all. [*READY* VIOLA *to enter* L. C.
LADY D. All. I read it in your face last night. You love your wife, Roy; it is good and right that you should. I honor and respect Alice; she will make you a true wife and a proud countess. You do love her, Roy?
ROY. Yes, mother; I do. I did not know how much until now, when I hear you praise her. This morning I shall write to Paisey or his wife, to inquire about Alice's birth. There is some mystery; I feel sure that she is nobly born.
LADY D. I agree with you, and we must discover the truth.
[*Knock at door* L. C.
ROY. Come in.

ENTER VIOLA, L. C., *simulating suppressed excitement.*

VIOLA (L. C.). Roy, something dreadful has happened! The countess has disappeared!

ROY (C., *puzzled*). Disappeared? [LADY DARRELL, R.

VIOLA. She is not in her room, nor did she sleep there last night. I think she has left the castle.

ROY (*carelessly*). She has gone for a walk. How can you be so absurd? She is about the grounds somewhere; she will be in directly.

LADY D. There is some mistake, surely.

VIOLA. That is not all; the castle was robbed last night.

[LADY DARRELL *and* ROY *start*. The butler says three of the gold cups, and several of the plates were stolen.

ROY (*impatiently*). What has that to do with my wife?

VIOLA. Much or little. The Darrell diamonds are gone.

LADY D. (*startled*). What are you saying?

VIOLA. And your guest, Count Jura, has disappeared too.

ROY (*in desperation*). Merciful Providence, Viola, what are you concocting?

VIOLA. A tragedy.

ROY. Speak plainly — what do you mean?

VIOLA. I mean that you have been robbed and deserted; they have fled together.

ROY. It is false! [VIOLA *pretends to be wounded*. Forgive me, Viola; I don't know what I am saying. I think I am mad. Oh, this is too horrible! It cannot be true!

VIOLA. Remember what you saw when we came upon them unexpectedly last night.

ROY. That is no proof; he had insulted her; she called upon me to resent the insult.

VIOLA (*quickly*). A subterfuge. She found herself trapped; her quick wit invented a means of escape. I'll warrant she is laughing now at the ease with which she imposed upon you.

ROY (*in despair*). And I thought her so pure and true!

VIOLA (*with sympathy*). Don't take it so badly; remember how she has disgraced you — think of her only as one utterly unworthy —

ROY. Stop, Viola, she is my wife. Had I not forgotten that, had I given her the love which was rightfully hers, the love for which she hungered, this would not have happened. No, it is I who am to blame.

VIOLA (*eagerly*). Do you intend to follow them?

ROY. I shall seek *him*, if I have to go to the end of the world.

LADY D. (*beseeching*). Roy, my son!

[*READY* DALE, *to enter* L. C.

ROY (*arms about his mother*). Don't grieve, mother; it is but another bitter blow; we shall survive it as we survived the other.

VIOLA (*crosses to* LADY DARRELL). Come, Lady Darrell; we know the worst now.

LADY D. (*up to door* L. C. *with* VIOLA; *turns to* ROY, *brokenly*). Heaven's will be done, my son.

ROY (*to* VIOLA). Viola, you will stay with my mother?

VIOLA. Until you bid me go. (*EXIT door* L. C., *with* LADY DARRELL.)

ROY. It is fate — the cup of happiness but raised to my lips, when it is dashed away!

ENTER DALE, *quickly, door* L. C.

DALE. Roy, I have just heard —

ROY. Spare me! (*Raises his hand to stop* DALE).

        [*READY* SIR GEOFFREY, *to enter door* L. C.

DALE. There is no time to mince matters. I have had all the particulars from the servants. It is suspected that the countess has eloped with Jura, but I tell you you are the victim of some horrible treachery.

ROY (*eagerly*). Why do you think so?

DALE (C.). I don't know; I feel it here. (*Hand on heart.*) A man, your guest, has disappeared; at the same time your wife is missing; some one tells you they have eloped, and you believe it. I knew or saw but little of the countess, but if all the scandal-tipped tongues this side of purgatory said she was false, I would tell them they lied.

ENTER SIR GEOFFREY, *hurriedly, door* L. C.

SIR GEOFFREY (L). Dale, I have been doing a little investigating on my own account. When the countess disappeared last night, she was dressed in a loose silk gown, and wore slippers; she hasn't taken a cloak or hat!

DALE (*to* ROY). What did I tell you? Does a woman elope dressed like that, when there is a stock of clothing hanging within reach?

ROY (L). How do you account for her absence?

DALE. In a dozen different ways. She may have been delirious and wandered away. She may have been carried off by that infernal Count Jura.

ROY. Abducted? Impossible!

SIR G. (*slowly*). I am not so sure that it would be impossible. Something happened last night that may have a bearing on the case. Listen. After we had all retired, I tried to think whom the countess reminded me of. The more I thought, the more firmly was I convinced that she bore a striking resemblance to some one of my family, but who, I could not fix in my mind. Well, I found that sleep was out of the question; so I rose quietly, dressed, slipped out of my window into the garden, and walked a long distance down the road. As I turned to retrace my steps, a cart came along, and it struck me then that it was rather late for farmers to be abroad ; but preoccupied as my mind was, I thought no more of it. Just as the cart was opposite me, I struck a match to light my cigar. The men seemed startled when they saw me. They whipped up the horse, and one of them said, " Hold her down ; " and now that I remember it, he didn't have any dialect, but spoke in remarkably good English.

DALE (*in a tone of conviction*). Roy Darrell, your wife was in that cart.

ROY (*gravely*). I believe it. What shall we do ?

DALE. Do ? Get detectives down here at once. Scour the country, trace these devils, until we land them in jail and rescue Lady Darrell.

ROY (*grasping* DALE'S *hand*). God bless you, Dale. You have given me hope.

SIR G. I'm off to order the horses. (*EXIT, door* L. C.)

ROY (*crosses to door*, L. C.). Come, Dale ; I shall never rest until I hold her in my arms. (*EXIT, door* L. C.)

DALE. It's funny how little we value a thing until we have lost it. (*EXIT, door* L. C.)   [*Flats are drawn off, disclosing* SCENE II. — *The vaults of the old abbey — a Gothic chamber will answer. See scene-plot for description. Lights half down.* JURA, *dressed roughly, as in Act I., is discovered* C., *looking at* ALICE, *who lies on the stage at his feet, as though he had just brought her in.*

ENTER MOTHER CRIPPS, R. 3 E.

JURA (*to* MOTHER CRIPPS). Here, I've brought something.

MOTHER CRIPPS. Something for me, George? (*She speaks in a cracked, high-pitched voice.*)

JURA. Yes ; something for you to look after.

MOTHER C. (*comes down* C. ; *sees* ALICE ; *in surprise*). A girl ?

JURA (L. C. ; *impressively*). A lady ; and as such you must treat her, or you will tell me the reason why.

MOTHER C. (R. C.). What have you brought her here for ?

JURA (*roughly*). That's my business, not yours. All you have to do is to wait on her ; see she has everything she wants. Kate can help you.

MOTHER C. (*examining* ALICE). You have drugged her ?

JURA. Yes.   [*READY* KATE, *to enter* L. 3 E.

MOTHER C. How long will she stay here?

JURA. As long as I find it convenient — two or three days perhaps. Long enough to let them search this neighborhood, and be looking farther away. Now, watch her carefully. I expect her to wake in a few minutes; give her some water; she may go off to sleep again. I must go back to Toby, bring in the swag, and close up the entrance. You shall have something for your pains.

MOTHER C. (*eagerly*). Diamonds? You promised me diamonds the next job, George.

JURA. You shall have them. Now, remember, look after her.
[ALICE *moves.*
She is moving. Where is Kate?

MOTHER C. (*nodding to* L.). Asleep in the next room.

JURA. Keep her there for to-night. (*EXIT,* R. 3 E.)

ENTER KATE, L. 3 E. *She comes quietly down* L., *looking at* ALICE.

KATE. Mother, who is this?

MOTHER C. (R. C.; *starts; sullenly*). It's a girl, as ye can see for yourself.

KATE (*crosses; catches* MOTHER CRIPPS *by the arm; imperiously*). Answer me at once, do you hear? Who brought her here — Toby or George?

MOTHER C. (*hesitates; sullenly*). Why, Toby, to be sure. As to who she is, I don't know any more than you do. She looks like a lady.

KATE (*gloomily, looking at* ALICE). She is very beautiful. (*To* MOTHER CRIPPS, *suspiciously*.) You swear you are speaking the truth? It was Toby who brought her?

MOTHER C. (*soothingly*). Deary me, of course I spoke the truth. What would I tell you a lie for?

KATE (*contemptuously*). For gold, or for diamonds.

MOTHER C. Sh! she is waking.

ALICE (*moans; turns uneasily*). Water, water! Davis, water!
[MOTHER CRIPPS *gives her water.*
(ALICE *raises herself up.*) Where am I? Davis, Davis, are you there? (*Looks about.*) Am I asleep? What place is this? (*Sees* KATE.) Who are you? Where am I?

KATE (*crossly*). You are with friends.

MOTHER C. (*soothingly*). You are quite safe, deary; lie down and rest again. Kate, go away; don't you see you frighten her? He will — I mean Toby will be angry.

KATE. I don't mind Toby's anger. (*Bitterly*.) Frightened, is she? Oh, I am sorry for her. But that will wear off; she will see a good deal of me; she'll get used to me in time, perhaps.
[*READY* JURA, *to enter* R. 3 E.

ALICE (*rising, kneels at* KATE'S *feet*). Oh, have pity, help me! I don't know what has happened to me — I can remember nothing clearly. I seem to have been asleep, but I feel, I am sure, something terrible has come to me. I am frightened at this gloomy place ; help me get away — you are a woman — you will help me!

MOTHER C. Come, come. (*Trying to take* ALICE'S *arm to lift her.*) You must lie down again and go to sleep. You will be ill.

ALICE (*pushes* MOTHER CRIPPS *away ; clings to* KATE). Oh, have pity, help me! Take me away out into the air! For Heaven's sake, help me!

KATE (*stoops down to raise* ALICE ; *hears* JURA *coming ; rises ; speaks coldly*). Here is some one coming who can help you. I can't plead to him.

> [ALICE *hears* JURA'S *footsteps,* R.; *rises, and turns toward door, hands outstretched.*

ENTER JURA, R. 3 E. *He comes* C. *toward* ALICE, *who recognizes him, and crouches away.*

JURA (C.). You are ill ; rest here a while, and you will — (*Attempts to take her hand.*)

JURA, C.

MOTHER CRIPPS, R.   ALICE, L. C.   KATE, L.

ALICE (*recoils from him*). Don't touch me! O Heaven, what terrible thing has happened to me?

> [JURA *starts to catch* ALICE.

KATE (*steps in front of him*). Leave her to me.

JURA. I will take care of her.

> [KATE *shakes her head ; supports* ALICE. *EXEUNT* KATE *and* ALICE, R. 3 E. *READY* TOBY, *to enter* R. 3 E.

JURA (*looks, and takes a step or two after them ; then turns toward* MOTHER CRIPPS). She will be kind to the other one?

MOTHER C. (R.). Yes ; Kate is a strange one, but she ain't cruel ; she thinks it's Toby's girl. I told her so. I thought it best.

JURA (L.). You did right. Though I don't care much — she must know sooner or later. I mean to make that golden-haired girl my wife.

MOTHER C. Do you, George? How will you do that? I see she wears a wedding-ring already.

JURA. Have you lived all these years, Mother Cripps, to learn from me that a ring does not make a marriage?

MOTHER C. Well, well, it's nothing to me. But what about the diamonds, George?

JURA. Toby is bringing them. Here he is. (*Down* R.)

ENTER TOBY, R. 3 E. NOTE: TOBY *can be made a very effective Cockney dialect part.*

TOBY. Halloo, Mother! What, all alone? (*Comes* C.; *puts bag carefully upon floor.*) Where's Kate?

MOTHER C. Kate? In there. (*Nods toward* L.) She's been out, doing her duty.

JURA. Where was that?

MOTHER C. Scouting around the Grange, a few miles from here — there's a lot of plate there, with a small fortune. It's the next crib to crack.

TOBY. Well, I think we've done enough in this neighborhood; we'd better slope. The whole country will be out on the hunt after carrying off this countess.

JURA. Well, this will be our last job. We will leave after that.   [*READY* KATE, *to enter* L. 3 E.

TOBY. Let's leave now. We'll be caught like rats in a trap in this place, some day. I won't have a finger in that job, George.

JURA. I am not afraid, my dear Toby, if you are. Courage, my friend; and remember, you join in the game at the Grange, I command you. (*Takes bag; crosses to table,* L.; *puts bag on table, and takes out cases of diamonds.*)

       [TOBY *mutters and crosses down* R. MOTHER CRIPPS
         goes behind table L.

(*Puts diamonds on table; to* MOTHER CRIPPS). Here, here's your share, Mother Cripps. (*Gives her a diamond ring; turning to* TOBY.) Toby, what will you have?

TOBY (*sullenly*). Nothing of that lot; give me the cups and plates.

JURA (*laughs sneeringly*). Toby, you're growing cowardly. Well, take the cups and plates; I keep the diamonds.

       [*EXIT* TOBY, *muttering*, R. 3 E. JURA *crosses* R., *examining diamonds* MOTHER CRIPPS *comes down* L. *from behind table.*

ENTER KATE, L. 3 E. *She stands in the doorway.*

MOTHER C. What will you do with the diamonds, George?

JURA. Take them abroad, and dispose of them there. (*Admiring the diamonds.*)

KATE (*aside*). Take them abroad? He is going away, and takes her with him. Coward! he forgets me.

JURA (*looks up; sees* KATE). What are you muttering about, Kate?

KATE. Nothing. (*Comes toward* C., *a little up stage.*) I was thinking of those diamonds.

JURA. Well, go into the vault and put one of your old dresses on the lady.

KATE (*coldly*). She may not wish to change her dress.

JURA. Tell her it is to help her escape

[KATE *looks at him sharply.*

(*Roughly.*) Do you hear me?

[*EXIT* KATE, *sullenly*, L. 3 E.; *READY to re-enter.*

(*Comes* C.; *looks after* KATE.) Mother Cripps, Kate is getting to be a nuisance. You must keep her in check, or look out for another berth.

MOTHER C. (*whining*). She's only a bit foolish, George. (*Coming toward* JURA.) I'll speak to her, and tell her you ain't pleased with her. She ain't a bit like me; she takes after her father.

JURA (*roughly*). Well, I can't be worried with her foolishness (*crosses* L.), and there's the end to it.

MOTHER C. I'll speak to her, George, I'll speak to her. Now, I must go to get some wood for the fire. (*EXIT*, R. 3 E.)

JURA. Well, you can speak to her or not; I'll be rid of you all before long. (*Retires up stage; lies down on rugs.*)

ENTER KATE, L. 3 E.

KATE (L. C.; *looks about cautiously; doesn't see* JURA; *looks off* L. 3 E.; *speaks as if looking at* ALICE; *bitterly*). Yes, she is here against her will; he has carried her away, drugged and insensible. Who is she? Her hands are white and soft. I will help her; my heart burns against her; she is in my power; yet I cannot do her any harm. It is he who shall suffer. He loves her; yes (*comes down* C.), there was a look on his face that he never gave me. He shall suffer. I will get her away — I will help her to escape. •

JURA (*has come down stage quietly; stands behind* KATE, *listening; at the end of her speech, he takes her by the throat*). So, you viper, you are plotting against me, are you? (*Choking her.*) Treacherous, eh?

KATE (*struggles away from him; throws him off, and stands panting* L. C.; *goes down toward* L. *corner*). Yes; treacherous, if you like; though it's not from you that such words should come, George Vaughn.

JURA (C.). Hush! Dare to breathe that name again, and I'll — (*Raises his hand as if about to strike her.*)

KATE. Kill me? (*Defiantly.*) Well, do it. What have I to

live for? You have treated me like dirt under your feet. (*Bitterly.*) Do you ever think of my degradation, of my suffering? And now you want to put another woman in my place!

[*READY* MOTHER CRIPPS, *with wood, to enter* R. 3 E.

JURA. I am in no mood for recrimination. Kate, I tell you plainly —

KATE. Have you forgotten all that you swore to me? Have you forgotten your promise that I should be your wife?

JURA (*coolly*). Yes. Come, Kate, don't be a fool. We have had our sunshine; it is gone. (*Coaxingly.*) But we needn't quarrel; let us be friends. I cannot do without you, Kate — I swear it!

KATE. Do you mean that?

JURA. Mean it? Of course I do. Come, give me your hand (*holds out his hand*); let us make up.

[KATE *shrinks away; then, as if a thought struck her, gives him her hand.*

Now you are my wise Kate once more. I want your help. This plate must be taken to London at once, and melted.

ENTER MOTHER CRIPPS *with wood*, R. 3 E. *She comes down* R.

Here, Mother Cripps, I want you to go down to London with Kate. She will take the plate to Moses to melt, and you will get the den ready for me. I will leave the lady there while I go abroad to dispose of the diamonds. I shall be gone only a week at most. Come, get ready to start.

[MOTHER CRIPPS *goes up* R., *puts wood on stage, gets shawl, etc.*

KATE (L.). And does she (*pointing* L. 3 E.), stay with us?

JURA. Yes, of course. (*EXIT* R. 3 E.)

[*READY* JURA *and* TOBY *to enter* R. 3 E.

KATE (*comes up* C., *looking after* JURA). He lies to my face. Traitor! coward! he thinks I am helpless, but I shall find a way. (*Defiantly.*) He shall soon learn what it is to break the heart of Kate Cripps. (*EXIT* L. 3 E., *READY to re-enter.*)

MOTHER CRIPPS (*comes down* C., *putting on shawl and hood, chuckling*). Well, well, I am going back to London, back to all my boys — my boys that earn the money for old Mother Cripps. I am glad to go. (*Crosses* L. C.)

ENTER JURA, R. 3 E., *followed by* TOBY. *ENTER* KATE, L. 3 E., *with hat and jacket on.*

JURA (C.). Ah, Kate, you are ready? You're a treasure. Here is the key of the house. Bill will meet you at the station.

Empty the sack (*puts diamonds, etc., into sack*), lock them away, you know where. Go to Moses, and tell him to get his melting-pot ready. I shall be in London in a couple of days.

TOBY (R.). How are ye going to get the loidy (*points L.*) to Lunnon? That'll be risky.

JURA. I have a very easy way of doing it, never fear.

KATE (L.; *points to ring on* MOTHER CRIPPS'S *finger*). George, have her take that off; it isn't safe.

JURA (*to* MOTHER CRIPPS). Yes, take it off.

> [MOTHER CRIPPS, L. C., *takes off ring sullenly, and gives it to* JURA.

Kate is wise. Be careful. Mother Cripps; be careful.

MOTHER C. (*sullenly*). Oh, I'm to be trusted.

JURA (*crosses down to* L. *corner*). Of course. Now, Kate, it's time to start. Remember all you have to do. You're always safe, my girl, always safe.

MOTHER C. Good-by. (*Crosses* R.; *laughs*). I'm off to Lunnon, and to my boys. (*EXIT* R. 3 E.)

KATE (*goes toward door* R. 3 E.; *stops and turns to* JURA; *appealingly*). George, don't go away to-day.

JURA (*frowns*). To-day? Why, Kate, how could I go, with the Grange plant on to-night? You are forgetting that.

KATE. Yes; I forgot that. Good-by.

TOBY (R.). Good-by, and good luck.

JURA. Good-by; be careful. [*EXIT* KATE, R. 3 E. (*Comes* C.; *looks after her*.) She's gone, thank Heaven. She's a nuisance.

TOBY. She's jealous of t'other one. I'd feel better if we was goin' to Lunnon ourselves.

JURA. I didn't think you were a coward, Toby.

TOBY (*sullenly*). Nor am I; I'm careful, that's all.

JURA (*sneers*). Careful?

TOBY. Yes, careful; we've got off safe after this job; let well enough alone. We've got enough swag.

JURA. We can't have too much. My mind is made up — everything is arranged. I shall go on with the job.

TOBY (*desperately*). Well, then, go on yourself. I won't be in it.

JURA (C.; *airily*). Oh, I think you will, Toby.

TOBY (*mocks his tone*). Oh, I think I won't, Georgie. (*Comes* R. *of* JURA.)

JURA (*puts his hand on* TOBY'S *shoulder; meaningly*). Then I shall inform Dan Wilkes. when I go up to town, that the man he is looking for, the man who murdered his wife, is none other than Tob —

TOBY (*in terror*). Hush! for Heaven's sake, hush! I'll go. curse you! May you never be in such a push yourself. (*Threateningly.*) Let the plant go on, and if the worst does come, I give you fair warning. Master George, you shall stand in the dock with me. I swear it!

[*READY* ALICE, *to enter* L. 3 E.

JURA (*laughs*). Don't get angry; the plant won't fail. (*Crosses toward table*, L.)

TOBY. And now for the diamonds. What's to become of them?

JURA (*turns; looks at* TOBY *quickly*). They are mine; I thought that was settled.

TOBY (*sneeringly*). And the other treasure (*pointing* L.), is she yours too?

JURA (*threateningly*). She is; have you any objections?

TOBY (*shrugs his shoulders; starts up* R. 3 E.; *turns*). You are coming with me to-night?

JURA. Of course. [*EXIT* TOBY, R. 3 E. (*Up* C., *looking after* TOBY.) To-night will see us separated for good and all, my friend. I am growing sick of your sulky ways. I leave you all for a dream of bliss, a life of happiness — after these gloomy vaults, sunshine, flowers, love. I never thought a woman lived who could move me so; but once away, alone, and in my power, all will go well. (*Noise* L. 3 E.) She is coming. (*Retires to* R. 3 E.)

ENTER ALICE, L. 3 E.

ALICE (*cautiously*). The gypsy girl told me I could escape in this dress; no one is here. O Mother in Heaven, look down upon me now, and guide me to safety. (*Starts up* R., *towards* 3 E; JURA *steps out;* ALICE *screams, and as* JURA *comes towards her, backs toward* L. C.)

JURA (C.; *mockingly*). Do not shrink from me, fair countess; I will do you no harm.

ALICE (L. C.; *desperately*). What is it that you want with me?

JURA. Nothing disagreeable, I hope; I wish to help you.

ALICE. To help me! Was it not through you that I came here? (*Disdainfully.*) Help me! Count Jura, what have I done that you should treat me in this shameful way?

[*READY* KATE, *to enter* R. 3 E.

JURA. Shameful — and you enjoying my hospitality? You insult our home (*waves his hand at surroundings*) and all its luxuries. Come, be friends. (*Takes a step toward her, hand outstretched.*)

ALICE (*shrinks from him*). Don't touch me! I loathe, I detest you ! You are a coward, to treat a woman as you have treated me. Let me go, this instant.

JURA. Go where ; back to the castle? That would be unwise, my lady. You would only exchange very comfortable quarters for an iron cage — in other words, you would be imprisoned for robbery.

ALICE (*puzzled*). Robbery ? Ah (*realizes*), I understand ; you are not a count, you are a thief, and this is your hiding-place.

JURA (*coolly*). You have guessed right. Yes (*saunters* R.), the castle has been robbed —

ENTER KATE, R. 3 E. *She remains up* R., *listening.*

robbed of its plate, of its diamonds, of its countess. Do you know what they think ? That we have taken the jewels and left the country together. You are branded as a thief. It is best that you know exactly how we stand. I have taken you — henceforth you are mine. (*Roughly.*) No screams — no weakness ! Listen, I shall flee from here to-night ; I shall leave the whole gang ; and for what? For love — love of you. We will start at once. I love you, and will not give you up. Come, give me your hand ; delays are dangerous ; delay means — (*Starts toward* ALICE.)

KATE (*comes down* C., *between* JURA *and* ALICE). Many awkward things.

JURA (*recoils, astonished*). Kate ! (*Roughly.*) What brings you here ?

KATE (C., *defiantly*). The fiend, perhaps. Ah, you thought to play me a trick. You should have known me better. (*Triumphantly.*) You have failed, George ; the game is mine.

JURA (R. ; *quickly draws revolver and shoots* KATE, *who screams and falls* C. JURA R. C., *behind* KATE, *bends over her just as he did over* CAPTAIN WYNDHAM *in first act.*) Curse you !

ALICE (L. C. ; *screams*). Ah, I know you now — you are the murderer of Captain Wyndham ! (*Points to* JURA, *who recoils in astonishment.*) [*Flash lights full up for Picture.*

PICTURE.

JURA.

KATE.   ALICE.

R. C.   L.

CURTAIN.

ACT IV. ˙

SCENE I.— A London street in 1 G. *As curtain rises,
ENTER* Mrs. Paisey, *with valise,* R., *followed by* Paisey,
carrying a carpet-bag; both arguing.

Mrs. Paisey (L.).   I tell you, Paisey, I'm not going to leave the
country until ye hev done it.

Paisey (R.).   But, Martha, jest think of the risk!

Mrs. P. (*contemptuously*).   Bah! you're a coward!

Paisey.   Well, ye may call me a coward, but I don't like to
do it.

Mrs. P. (*arguing*).   I tell ye, there's no danger.

Paisey (*not convinced*).   Well, if ye don't think there's any
danger, do it yerself.

Mrs. P. (*looks at him quickly in disgust*).   That's just like a
man, — trying to shift everything onto the poor, weak woman.

Paisey.   Well, it don't take much strength to carry a little piece
of jewellery to the pawn-shop.

Mrs. P. (*decidedly*).   You're the man; it's your place to do it.

Paisey (*trying to mollify her*).   Well, wait till we get to
America.

Mrs. P. (*positively*).   You're a fool!   Here we are jest goin'
to get out of the country; and if ye pawn it here, and anything
does come of it, why, when they look fer us, we're gone thousands
of miles across the ocean.   No, here's the place to do it, and do
it ye must.

Paisey (*resigned*).   Well, if I must, I must; but it seems like
stealin'.

Mrs. P. (*almost screams*).   Stealin'?   Do ye know who it
belongs to?

Paisey.   Why, to the child, of course.

Mrs. P.   To the child, indeed!   And pray, what's to pay us for
her keep all these years?

Paisey (*meekly*).   Why, the money her mother give us.

Mrs. P. (*tosses her head*).   Wasn't enough to pay for her
clothes.

Paisey (*surprised*).   Why, it was five hundred pounds!

Mrs. P.   Well, if it was; look at all the years I've given her a
mother's love and care.

PAISEY (*doggedly*). Yes ; and the whip.

MRS. P. (*snappishly*). Shut up ! Now, for the last time, will ye go pledge the locket ?

PAISEY (*resigned*). Yes ; I guess I'll do anything for peace. Where shall I say I got it ?

MRS. P. (*thinks a moment*). Why, say a rich lady give it to ye for stopping her runaway horses.

PAISEY (*looks at her*). Yer mighty ready with lies.

MRS. P. (*snaps him up*). Will ye shut up ? Go find the shop ; I'll wait fer ye at the tavern. And, mind ye (*warningly*), don't be long. (*Takes carpet-bag from* PAISEY, *and EXIT* L. I E.)

[*READY* TOBY *to enter* L.

PAISEY (R. C.; *looks cautiously around ; takes locket from pocket ; looks at it*). Well, the old woman can say what she likes, but to my mind it's little short of stealin'. How well I remember the night the poor lady knocked at our door. How my breath almost left me when I opened the door and found her lyin' on the step, with her wee baby in her arms ! We took her in, but she was too far gone to tell us anything — just lay there as white as death, with her great eyes starin' as if askin' for help. When all at onct the old woman recognized her, and went to scoldin' and jawin' at her for runnin' away, and then comin' back with her shame. She just managed to gasp out there was no shame ; she was a wife ; her baby's father was a nobleman. Then, as if it was too much for her, she lay back and died. How the old woman did go on about havin' the body in the house, and what to do with the brat, as she called it ; but she soon changed her mind when she found the roll of bank-notes and this locket. Well, the child has plenty now, and she will never miss this little bauble. (*Stands looking at locket.*) [*READY* POLICEMAN *to enter* L.

ENTER TOBY L., *during* PAISEY'S *speech ; walks cautiously over to him ; looks over his shoulder ; sees locket ; whistles with surprise.*

(*Turns quickly ; puts locket·in pocket.*) Well, what do ye want ? TOBY (L. C.; *sulkily*). Nothin'. (*Coaxingly.*) Now, don't get mad, old bloke. I jest couldn't help whistlin' when I see that bloomin' locket. All studded over with diamonds. It's a beauty ! PAISEY (*defiantly*). Well, it's mine.

[*READY* ROY *and* DALE *to enter* L.

TOBY. Well, I didn't say as how it wasn't. (*Insinuatingly.*) Blow my bloomin' eyeballs, but I've a friend as would be glad to see that gem !

PAISEY (*eagerly*). Have ye ? Well, that's just what I want to find — I want to sell it.

TOBY. Ye does? (*Quickly.*) Sh!

[POLICEMAN *ENTERS* L., *crosses in front, eying them suspiciously, and EXIT* R.

PAISEY (*aside, looking after* POLICEMAN. *fearfully*). I'm sure he knows something is wrong, by the way he looked at us.

TOBY (*crosses* R., *in front of* PAISEY, *looking after* POLICEMAN; *aside*). That bloomin' peeler looked suspicious. (*Turns to* PAISEY.) I say, if yer want to find a nice, obligin' gentleman what will buy yer jewellery, why, come along with me. I'll show yer his shop.

PAISEY. You're very kind. Is it far? I haven't much time.

TOBY. Just down the way a bit. (*Points* R.) Come with me. (*Takes* PAISEY'S *arm.*)

[*They EXEUNT* R., *talking ad lib. as they go.*

ENTER ROY *and* DALE, L.

DALE (L.). My dear Roy, for Heaven's sake, try to have patience.

ROY (R.). Patience? How can you preach patience at such a time? (*He is walking back and forth excitedly.*)

[*READY* SIR GEOFFREY, KATE, *and* VIOLA, *to enter* R.

DALE. But, old fellow, your brain will give way under this strain. Think, you have been on the go for two nights and days, with scarcely a bite to eat, and not a wink of sleep.

ROY. I feel as if I shall never sleep again. I did not know how I loved her, until I lost her.

DALE (*drily*). That's usually the way. (*Cheerfully.*) But cheer up, old chap, we shall find her, I feel sure of it. The whole police force is on the lookout for Jura; the docks and railway stations are all guarded by detectives. He cannot leave London. He is caught like a rat in a trap, and sooner or later we shall lay our hands upon him.

ROY. But in the meantime, Alice — Alice is in his power. What may he not do? I shall go mad. (*Goes* L., *to* DALE.)

DALE (*looking* R.). By jove, look! Here comes Sir Geoffrey — and who is this he has with him?

ENTER SIR GEOFFREY, R., *leading* KATE, *whose head is bandaged.* VIOLA *follows them. She is veiled, and keeps in the background, listening to what the others say.*

SIR GEOFFREY (C.). Good news! Good news!

SIR GEOFFREY, C.

VIOLA, R.   KATE, R. C.   ROY, L. C.   DALE, L.

ROY. Quick! In Heaven's name, tell it.

[*READY* PAISEY, *to enter* R.

SIR G. After you had started for London, this poor girl revived. I questioned her, and she has told me all, — how the villain shot her down, then escaped, taking your wife with him. But we shall soon have him in our power, and your wife in your arms, for this girl will lead us to his hiding-place.

ROY (*to* KATE). You know it?

KATE. Yes; the Beggars' Paradise.

VIOLA (*aside*). I, too, know where it is. I must warn my brother. (*EXIT, quickly*, R.)

ROY. Let us lose no time.

DALE. Hold on; we must have a sufficient force of police, first.

ROY. I shall wait for no police; you and Sir Geoffrey can follow with them.

ENTER PAISEY, R., *talking as he comes.*

PAISEY. Oh, I've been robbed, I've been robbed! (*Crosses past* KATE *and* SIR GEOFFREY; *to* ROY.) O Lord Darrell, I've been robbed! You will help me, won't you, my lord?

SIR. G. (*impatiently*). My good man, we are sorry for you, but we have important matters to attend to; you must ask the police to help you.

PAISEY. Oh, I asked a policeman down the street; he said he'd find the thief, but I know it's no use. Oh, whatever shall I tell the old woman?

ENTER POLICEMAN, R., *dragging* TOBY; *he brings* TOBY *to* R. C., *crossing in front of* KATE.

(*Sees* TOBY; *crosses quickly to* SIR GEOFFREY.) Oh, there he is; they've caught him! (*To* TOBY.) You rascal, to rob me! Give me my property!

KATE, R. C.

POLICEMAN. TOBY. PAISEY. SIR G. ROY. DALE, L.

TOBY (*sullenly*). Your property? I ain't got no property o' yourn.

PAISEY. Yes, ye have — that locket. Give it up.

TOBY. Will you let me go if I do? You won't appear ag'in me?

PAISEY (*eagerly*). No, no; I won't appear. Jest give me the locket.

TOBY (*gives locket*). Well, there it is.

[PAISEY *holds locket in* L. *hand.*

SIR G. (*sees locket; very much excited; takes it from* PAISEY'S *hand.*) Where did you get this?

PAISEY (*confused*). Why, I — I —

SIR G. (*sternly*). No lies — I know this locket. Tell the truth, or I will hand you over to the police.

PAISEY (*imploringly*). O Sir Geoffrey, please don't; I'll tell ye all. My wife took it from the neck of a poor lady as died in our house, where she came asking for shelter for herself and her baby.

SIR G. She is dead?

PAISEY. Yes, Sir Geoffrey.

SIR G. (*quickly*). And the baby?

PAISEY. My wife and I raised her as if she was our own.

SIR G. (*impatiently*). Where is she now?

PAISEY. She is Lord Darrell's wife.

SIR G. Merciful Heaven! (*To* ROY.) Lord Darrell, you need feel no shame on the score of your wife's origin. She comes of a family as good as your own. (*Looks at locket.*) She is the daughter of my eldest son who ran away and married a poor girl. He died abroad. I have searched for years for his widow and her child. The mother is dead, but I have found the child by means of this locket. (*Thinks suddenly.*) Found, did I say? I had forgotten — she is in that villain's power.

PAISEY (*appealingly to* SIR GEOFFREY). Can I go, my lord?

SIR G. Yes, go; and be thankful that I can find some excuse to forgive you for robbing the dead.

PAISEY. I'll reform. I'm leaving for America. (*Crosses in front of* ROY *and* DALE, *to* L.) Thank you, my lord, thank you. (*EXIT* L. I E.)

SIR G. (*to* POLICEMAN). Lead us to the nearest police-station.

[POLICEMAN, *with* TOBY, *crosses in front of* KATE *to* R. *corner.*

(*To* ROY *and the others.*) Come! (*Crosses in front of* KATE *to* R. C.)   [KATE *comes* C.

KATE, C.

POLICEMAN *and* TOBY, R.   ROY, L. C.

SIR GEOFFREY, R. C.   DALE, L.

ROY (*taking* KATE *by the hand*). No, this girl and I will go on ahead; you can follow with the officers. *Crosses in front of* DALE, *with* KATE, *to* L.)

DALE (C.). Wait for the police; it's safer.

ROY. Safer! Do you suppose I can think of safety with my wife in that villain's clutches? I am going to her rescue, if it takes the last drop of blood in my veins! (*To* KATE.) Come! (*Drags her off* L.)

SIR G. To the police-station!

[*EXEUNT* POLICEMAN, TOBY, SIR GEOFFREY, *and* DALE, R. I E. *Flats are drawn off, disclosing*

SCENE II. — The " Beggars' Paradise " — a rough kitchen will answer. For setting, see scene-plot. Lights half down. MOTHER CRIPPS *is DISCOVERED seated at table* L., *peeling potatoes. She croons constantly. On the table is a bottle of whiskey, from which she takes an occasional drink. READY* FOUR SUPERS *and* JURA, *to enter* C.

MOTHER CRIPPS. My boys will soon be home to supper. Ah, ha, good boys; they bring the old woman money, he, he, he! They always bring her money. When they can't steal, they beg; but they always bring money. So they must have their supper — good boys, good boys! (*Knock at door; she starts up.*) Who's there?

VOICE (*outside*). Open, Mother.

MOTHER C. He, he, he! the boys — the boys with money. (*Opens door* C.)

ENTER FOUR SUPERS, C. *One has a shade over his eyes, and wears a placard,* Help the Blind ; *another has a wooden leg; another carries a pair of crutches; another has one arm concealed within his shirt. When they are inside, they take out arm, throw away shade, wooden leg, placard, crutches, etc., up stage near steps, all laugh. She bolts the door.*

Good boys, good boys! Well, what have ye got for the old woman? [*One after another they give her coins, etc.* (*To one.*) Good, good! (*To another.*) Bah, that isn't so good! Trade is bad — well, go lie down till I get supper. [SUPERS *lie down around rear of stage.* (*Goes to table,* L.; *takes a drink from bottle; sits down to peel potatoes; muttering.*) Trade is bad — trade is bad! [*Knock at* C. *door.* Who's there?

JURA (*outside*). It is I, Mother. Come, hurry! [MOTHER CRIPPS *goes up and unbolts the door.*

ENTER JURA, C. *He comes down* R. C. MOTHER CRIPPS *closes and bolts the door.*

MOTHER C. Well, George?

JURA. Well, what?

MOTHER C. (*coming down* C.). Any news of Kate?

JURA (*roughly*). Yes; she was shot by the police after we got away from the abbey.

MOTHER C. (*screams*). What! My Kate, my daughter shot? (*In a fury.*) Curses on the bloodhounds, to shoot down a girl! Oh, I'll be even with them, curse them all!

JURA. Be careful of your curses; keep them for some other time. I want you to get Nathan here to-night.

MOTHER C. What for, George?

[*READY* ALICE, *to enter* L. 3 E.

JURA. Sh! (*Lays hand upon her arm; in a low tone.*) I have the diamonds to sell him.

[MOTHER CRIPPS *chuckles, and nods her head gleefully.* Where's the girl?

MOTHER C. (*points* L.). In there.

JURA. Bring her here.

MOTHER C. What are you going to do with her?

JURA (*roughly*). I am going to tame her — then I'll take her abroad.

MOTHER C. (*warningly*). Be careful, George. Many a good man has been ruined by a pretty face.

JURA. Attend to your own affairs; bring her here. (*Points to door* L., *then goes* R.)

MOTHER C. Have it your own way, have it your own way! (*Goes to door* L. *and unbolts it; EXIT; comes back, leading* ALICE, *who is in rags.*)

JURA. How beautiful she is, even in rags! Good-evening, Lady Darrell.

ALICE (C., *with dignity*). By what right do you keep me a prisoner here?

JURA (R.). By right of might.

[MOTHER CRIPPS R. *of table, listening.*

ALICE (*commanding*). I demand that you set me free at once.

JURA. What! Where do you wish to go — to your friends?

ALICE (*sadly*). Friends? I have no friends.

JURA (*mockingly*). Perhaps you wish to return to your husband — your loving husband, who is so taken up with Miss Vaughn that he hasn't found time to hunt for you. Why, I'll wager they are even now planning their marriage, glad that you are out of their way.

ALICE (*scarcely knowing what she says*). They cannot marry, I am his wife.

JURA (*laughs*). Oh, you mean you *were* his wife; you seem to forget there is a divorce court in England. Remember what I told you of the robbery? I took good care to make it appear that you had stolen the diamonds and eloped with me. Lord Darrell will find that sufficient grounds for a divorce, I fancy.

ALICE (*draws herself up*). You coward — to rob, and then attempt to throw suspicion upon an innocent woman! My husband invited you to his house; you were his guest. He treated you as his friend, little knowing that he was harboring a common thief — a murderer!

JURA (*angrily*). Take care!

ALICE (*fearlessly*). It is the truth; you are worse than the lowest of criminals, — you are a traitor! a dog that bit the hand that fed it!

JURA (*threatening*). You shall repent those words!

MOTHER C. Leave her to me. (*Starts at ALICE.*)

[ALICE *screams and shrinks from her.*

JURA (*motions* MOTHER CRIPPS *back*). No; stand off. (*To* ALICE.) Now, listen to me. We leave this place to-morrow forever; I shall take you to a foreign country. You can go quietly if you will; if not, it will be the worse for you. I have made up my mind to take you, and go you shall. If you go peaceably, I promise you that as soon as Lord Darrel gets his divorce, I will marry you.

ALICE. Marry *you!* Never! Were you to torture me until the last breath left my body, with that breath I would refuse! You are the most contemptible of villains, — a hypocrite who lacks the courage to appear in his true colors, but masquerades as a gentleman, so that he may hide from his unsuspecting victims what he really is, — a thief!

JURA (*in a rage*). Mother Cripps, put her in the black hole! We'll see if a few hours alone with the rats won't tame her. (*Up to door* R.) [MOTHER CRIPPS *starts at her;* ALICE *screams.*

ALICE (*in terror*). No, not that!

JURA (*laughs*). In with her! (*EXIT door* R.)

[*READY* ROY *to enter* C.

MOTHER C. (*seizes* ALICE *by wrist, and throws her around* L.; ALICE *sinks upon floor up near* L. *door.*) Here, none of that. (*Looks at her.*) Ye're not faintin', ye're only shammin'. (*Looks at her again; kicks her.*) I believe she has fainted. (*Goes to table, gets bottle, and is about to give* ALICE *some whiskey; stops.*) No, no; she'll come to all right — I can't waste good whiskey. (*Drinks from bottle; sits at table, peeling potatoes; takes another drink; is getting drunk; mutters to herself.* NOTE: *a great deal can be made of this scene, if the old woman plays it slowly, talking and muttering ad lib., taking an occasional pull at the bottle, etc.*) Get up from there! I've got to get my boys' suppers. D'ye hear me? Get up out of that. (*Drinks.*) I'll wager ye'll get up if I come to ye. (*Drinks.*) D'ye hear me? Get up out of that. (*Rises from table; steadies herself; goes to* ALICE; *kicks and shakes her.*) Get up, I say!

[ALICE *revives gradually.*

Get up, I say!

ALICE (*rises, assisted by* MOTHER CRIPPS; *pleadingly*). No, no ; don't put me in the black hole !

MOTHER C. Ye're to go into the black hole — it's orders. Come on, I say. (*Drags* ALICE, *who begs to be released, talking ad lib. EXIT door* L.)

> [*When they get off, noise of a blow is heard, and* ALICE *screams. Knock heard at door* C.

(MOTHER CRIPPS *comes out from door* L.) Who's there ?

ROY (*outside*). Me. Mother ; open the door.

MOTHER C. That voice sounds strange. (*Bolts* L. *door ; goes up, unbolts and opens* C. *door.*)

ENTER ROY C., *disguised as a beggar.*

(*Stops* ROY *on steps.*) I don't know you. Who are you ?

> [*READY* JURA *and* VIOLA, *to enter* R. 3 E. *and* C.

ROY (*quickly*). A new boarder. Mother ; the cops are after me. See, I have money ; hide me, and I'll pay you well. (*Jingles handful of coins.*)

MOTHER C. Well, if ye've money, and the police are after ye, I guess ye're all right ; come in.

> [ROY *comes down steps ; looks about stage.*

(*She bolts* C. *door, and comes down* L. *of* ROY.) Now, give me the money. [ROY *gives her money.* Go lie down till supper's ready.

> [ROY *starts toward* L. *door ; crosses in front of* MOTHER CRIPPS, *who catches him by the arm.*

No, no ; come away — ye mustn't go there. Lie down here. (*Points up stage where* SUPERS *are lying.*)

> [ROY *goes up stage and lies down.*

He, he, he ! A new boarder. More money — more money for the old woman. (*Goes toward table.*) [*Knock at* C. *door.* (*Stops ; listens in fear.*) Who's there ? Maybe it's another new boarder. Who's there ?

VIOLA (*outside*). Open the door, quick !

MOTHER C. A woman ! (*Goes up* C. *to foot of steps.*) Who do ye want to see ?

VIOLA (*outside*). George. Open quick — quick, do you hear ?

MOTHER C. Of course I hear. Wait a minute. (*Goes to* R. *door and calls.*) George !

JURA (*outside* R.). Well, what is it ?

MOTHER C. Come here !

ENTER JURA, R. 3 E.

There's a woman at the door, askin' fer ye. (*Points to* C. *door.*)

JURA. A woman ? (*Crosses in front of* MOTHER CRIPPS, *who*

drops down L., *and goes quickly to* C. *door*.) Who are you, and what do you want?

VIOLA (*outside*). It's I; I want to see you.

JURA. Viola! (*Unbolts and opens* C. *door*.)

ENTER VIOLA *quickly,* C. *She comes down steps to* C. JURA *bolts* C. *door, and comes down* R. *of* VIOLA.

VIOLA. George, you must escape — the police know your hiding-place — they may be here at any moment.

JURA. The Devil! How did they discover it?

VIOLA. Kate —   [*READY* ALICE *to enter* L. 3 E.

JURA (*puts his hand over her mouth*). Hush! (*Takes her to* R. *corner*.) Now, tell me; speak low.

VIOLA. That girl Kate told Sir Geoffrey and Roy. I followed and overheard her.

JURA. She isn't dead?

VIOLA. No — quick, George — escape while there is time.

JURA. You are right, (*Crosses in front of* VIOLA, *to* C.; *to* MOTHER CRIPPS.) Mother, get the girl.

      [MOTHER CRIPPS *starts* L., *unbolts door, and EXIT* L. 3 E.

VIOLA (R.; *in alarm*). George, you surely won't try to carry her off?

JURA (C.). Certainly; I wouldn't give her up now if it cost me my life.

VIOLA. But it will be too great a risk.

JURA. Do you want me to leave her for Roy Darrell?

VIOLA (*vindictively*). You are right — take her.

ENTER MOTHER CRIPPS, L. 3 E. *dragging* ALICE, *who struggles.*

JURA (R. C.; *takes hold of* ALICE). Come, Lady Darrell, we won't wait for to-morrow — we start to-night.

ALICE (C.). I will not go with you.

      [VIOLA, R.   MOTHER CRIPPS, *down* L.

JURA. I say you must!

ROY (*jumps down stage; throws* JURA *off* R.; *stands between him and* ALICE). I say she shall not!

JURA (*surprised*). Who are you?

ROY (*throws off disguise*). Roy Darrell!

Steps, C.

    BEGGARS.   BEGGARS

        ROY.

    JURA.   ALICE.

R. VIOLA.   MOTHER CRIPPS, L.

  JURA } *together*. { The Devil!
  VIOLA }   { Roy!

ALICE.   Roy! My husband!

JURA.   Up, men, up!   [*All the* BEGGARS *have risen.*
Seize that man; he is a police spy!
                              [BEGGARS *seize* ROY, *who struggles.*
Bind him!

> [BEGGARS *tie* ROY.   ALICE *tries to help him.*   MOTHER
> CRIPPS *seizes her; struggle; forces* ALICE *off* L. 3 E.,
> *and bolts door.*

Tie him to that post!
          [BEGGARS *tie* ROY *to post at steps*, C.   *Work this quickly.*

JURA (*laughs; to* ROY).   You came for your wife; you found
her; but you shall see me carry her away, (*Starts toward* L. *door.*)

VIOLA (*stops him, in terror*).` No, no, George; don't attempt
it! (*Lays hand upon his arm.*)   Save yourself — don't let your
blind infatuation ruin your chance of escape.

MOTHER C. (L.).   Remember what I told you about a pretty
face.   [JURA *stands* C., *undecided.*

VIOLA (*appealingly*).   Come, George, you have the diamonds,
be satisfied. Am I not leaving him? Come.

JURA.   Very well, I'll do as you ask. (*Points to* C. *door.*)

> [VIOLA *ascends steps, unbolts door, and stands waiting*
> *for* JURA.

(*To* ROY.)   Curse you, Roy Darrell! I'm taking the Darrell diamonds, see? (*shows case*), but I'm leaving behind the most price-
less gem of all. (*Points to* L. *door.*)   But if I don't possess it,
neither shall you. (*To* MOTHER CRIPPS.)   Do you want revenge
on the man who killed your daughter? Well, you can have it —
there he is. (*Points to* ROY.)

MOTHER C.   He?

JURA.   Yes, he.

MOTHER C. (*takes knife from bosom*).   I'll kill him!

JURA (*raises his hand to stop her*).   That is too easy a death.
Listen. The police are coming — we must leave this den forever
— burn it — let him roast — there's revenge for you.

MOTHER C.   I'll do it! I'll do it!

JURA.   Off with you, men.!
                    [BEGGARS *EXEUNT up steps, and off* C.
(*Hesitates*).   How can I leave her!

VIOLA.   Come!   [*READY* ALICE, *to enter* L. 3 E.

JURA (*starts up* C.; *to* ROY).   Good-by, Lord Darrell. Some
people say there's no hell, but when these old timbers get started,
you'll think differently. Would you like to know who killed Captain Wyndham? I did it. Yes, it was I, but the stain is on your
name, — the stain of blood. (*Laughs; goes up steps to* C. *door.*)
                    [*EXIT* VIOLA, C., *READY to re-enter.*

Good-by, Lord Darrell, and a pleasant journey to hell. (*EXIT,* c., *READY to re-enter.*)

MOTHER C. (L.). So you killed my girl? Curse you, I'll make a good warm fire for you. (*Gets candle from table* L., *and holds it in front of his face.*) Oh, you're very brave! But when the flames creep upon you, when you see your last minutes come, when your throat is parched and dry — just think of my poor girl, my girl, my girl, that ye killed, killed! But I'm going to kill you, he, he, he! (*Starts to door* R.) Yes, I'm going to make ye a bonfire, he, he, he! (*EXIT,* R. 3 E.)

> [ROY *struggles to free himself.*

RE-ENTER JURA, c.

JURA. I can't do it — I can't leave her. (*Crosses to* L. *door; unbolts it; EXIT,* L. 3 E.; *RE-ENTERS with* ALICE, *forcing her* c.) Come, come, my beauty. I'll take you if all the police in England stand in the way.

ALICE. Let me go! Let me go!

> [*They struggle and talk ad lib.;* ALICE *breaks away*
>   *from him and runs around table,* L.; *he follows to*
>   *table;* ALICE *gets knife that* MOTHER CRIPPS *used*
>   *for peeling potatoes.*

Stand off — or, as there is a heaven above, I will kill you!

> [JURA *stands at bay.*

ROY (*has succeeded in getting gag off*). Alice, Alice, cut these ropes.

> [*She runs quickly to* ROY; *cuts ropes. READY to en-*
>   *ter,* MOTHER CRIPPS R. 3 E.; DALE, SIR GEOFFREY,
>   KATE, *and two* POLICEMEN, C.

(*To* JURA.) Now, you cur, it is your life or mine! (*Throws off coat.*)

JURA (*throws off coat*). So be it; the man that wins gets the prize. (*Points to* ALICE.)

> [JURA *and* ROY *have a fist fight ad lib.; at last they*
>   *clinch and roll over down stage,* JURA *getting* ROY
>   *under.* ALICE *picks up* BEGGAR'S *crutch and strikes*
>   JURA *on the head; he falls* R.

ALICE. Come, Roy, come! (*Gives him her hand and assists him to his feet.*)

> [ALICE *and* ROY *start up* C. JURA *rises on one knee,*
>   *draws pistol, and shoots just as they reach the foot of*
>   *the steps.*

JURA. You sha'n't escape me! (*Shoots.*)

ENTER Viola, c. *She receives* Jura's *bullet, staggers, and falls up* r. c. *at foot of steps. Fire (red fire) off* r. 3 e. *ENTER* Mother Cripps r. 3 e.; *she goes* r. c. *ENTER* Dale, c.; *he comes down and disarms* Jura, *who is about to fire again. ENTER* Sir Geoffrey, Kate, *and two* Policemen, c. *One officer goes off* r. 3 e. *to extinguish fire; the other handcuffs* Jura. *Work this very rapidly.*

Viola, *up* r. c.
Mother Cripps, r. c.

Policeman.   Dale.   Roy.   Alice.
r., Jura.   Kate, c.   Sir Geoffrey, l.

Kate (*to* Jura).   George, I swore to be even with you; I have kept my oath.

Roy (*to* Sir Geoffrey).   Sir Geoffrey, there is the murderer of Captain Wyndham.

Dale (*raises* Viola's *veil*).   Why, this is Viola Vaughn!

Alice.   Yes; she is the sister of George Vaughn, whom you knew as Count Jura.

Dale (*picks up case of diamonds*, r. c.).   And, by Jove, here are the Darrell diamonds!   (*Gives them to* Roy.)   Roy, you are fortunate in recovering them.   (*Goes up* c.)

> [Kate *goes a little* r., *looking at* Jura, *who glowers at them all.*

Roy (*takes* Alice's *hand*).   I am indeed fortunate, for I have recovered the most precious of all gems, — My Lady Darrell.

> [*Just as the curtain is coming down,* Mother Cripps *tries to escape up* c. Dale *catches her by the ear, and leads her down* l. *to position for curtain.*

PICTURE.

Viola.

Policeman.
          Kate.   Roy.   Alice.   Sir Geoffrey.
r., Jura.   Mother Cripps.   Dale, l.

CURTAIN.